Rebecca Winters has written over forty-five books
for Harlequin Romance® and is an
internationally bestselling author. Her wonderfully
unique, sparkling stories continue to be immensely
popular with readers around the world.

Praise for

REBECCA WINTERS:

About *The Prince's Choice*

"Rebecca Winters…is pure magic."
—*Romantic Times*

About *Claiming His Baby*

"Rebecca Winters creates an extraordinary tale with a
majestic setting…and a strong emotional conflict."
—*Romantic Times*

WHAT WOMEN WANT!

It could happen to you...

Every woman has dreams—deep desires, all-consuming passions, or maybe just little everyday wishes! In this brand-new miniseries from Harlequin Romance® we're delighted to present a series of fresh, lively and compelling stories by some of our most popular authors—all exploring the truth about what women *really* want.

Step into each heroine's shoes as we get up close and personal with her most cherished dreams...big *and* small!

- Is she a high-flying executive...but all she wants is a baby?
- Has she met her ideal man—if only he wasn't her new boss...?
- Is she about to marry, but is secretly in love with someone else?
- Or does she simply long to be slimmer, more glamorous, with a whole new wardrobe?

Whatever she wants, each heroine finds happiness on her own terms—and unexpected romance along the way. And she's about to discover whether Mr. Right is the answer to her dreams—or if he has a few questions of his own!

This month enjoy *The Forbidden Marriage* by Rebecca Winters.

And look out for more stories in the WHAT WOMEN WANT! miniseries, coming soon!

THE FORBIDDEN MARRIAGE
Rebecca Winters

WHAT WOMEN WANT!
It could happen to you...

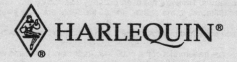

HARLEQUIN®

TORONTO • NEW YORK • LONDON
AMSTERDAM • PARIS • SYDNEY • HAMBURG
STOCKHOLM • ATHENS • TOKYO • MILAN • MADRID
PRAGUE • WARSAW • BUDAPEST • AUCKLAND

ISBN 0-373-03768-6

THE FORBIDDEN MARRIAGE

First North American Publication 2003.

CHAPTER ONE

MICHELLE HOWARD had just reached the second floor of her brother's Spanish-styled home in Riverside, California, when she saw her niece Lynette come out of the guest bedroom at the other end of the hall.

As soon as their eyes met, the eighteen year old brunette jumped. ''Aunt Michelle—what are you doing here?''

Michelle had probably frightened her niece who'd thought no one else was in the house besides Zak. Maybe that was the reason she'd sounded faintly accusatory just now.

''I was about to ask you the same question. Your mom said you had classes at college this morning.''

''Only one on Thursdays. It starts at eleven.''

Michelle glanced at her watch. ''Considering the heavy traffic, you'd better hurry if you want to get there on time.''

Lynette's pretty features hardened. ''I think I can manage my own life, thank you.''

Both Graham and Sherilyn had been complaining about their only daughter's change of attitude. It had come on over the summer. According to them she'd turned into someone defensive and difficult.

After this experience Michelle was beginning to understand what they meant. Lynette was behaving like a different girl. Michelle had never known her to be outright rude before.

"Forgive me, honey. I didn't mean anything by it. I'm sorry." With two ice bags and her blood pressure case tucked in one arm, she gave her niece a hug with the other, but Lynette barely reciprocated.

Puzzled, Michelle stepped back. Looping a strand of neck length ash blond hair behind her ear she said, "Your mother asked me to come over and check up on your uncle Zak while she did some grocery shopping."

Her niece's expression remained mutinous. "I *am* capable of waiting on him."

"I know. It's just that she's an anxious sister who wanted my medical assessment of her brother's condition this morning."

"He wouldn't be out of the hospital if he weren't getting better," Lynette said on a sarcastic note. "I'm almost nineteen, but everyone around here still thinks of me as an adolescent. You can be damn sure my parents never treated Zak like this!" Her brown eyes flashed in anger.

Michelle winced because she'd never heard Lynette so upset she'd swear in front of her. "I think it has more to do with the fact that your uncle Zak was already nine years old when my brother married your mom."

Even at nine, Zak had been a law unto himself. Michelle remembered back to those early days when her brother Graham had worked so hard to win Sherilyn's aloof younger brother around without coming across like a heavy handed stepfather type.

It had paid off. They had a great relationship as brothers-in-law now.

"Why do you insist on calling him my uncle? There's no blood tie between us."

Lynette, Lynette.

Her niece's bizarre behavior was finally beginning to make sense. The stretch from teen to adult could be a very confusing, painful time.

"Come on, Aunt Michelle. You know it's true. First his birth parents abandoned him and he lived in foster homes. Then Mom's parents adopted him and then they got killed. By the time I started kindergarten, Zak was already in high school. I hardly ever saw him."

"Nevertheless he's your uncle, and that makes him a member of your family," Michelle reminded her. "After Graham married your mom, they raised him and me with all the love two people possibly could. Zak and I were so lucky to have an older brother and sister who provided a stable home for us with both of our parents dead."

Naturally Sherilyn had wanted to bring her brother home to convalesce after his accident at the construction site. Michelle supposed that like anyone just out of the hospital, Zak was probably craving a little TLC about now.

Knowing how fiercely independent he was, this was a good way to avoid the ministrations of a number of women who, according to Sherilyn, hoped to be *the one*. However Zak hadn't shown signs of wanting to settle down yet.

No doubt he didn't want any of them to see him in his weakened condition. Michelle had nursed enough men young and old in her career to understand that part of the male psyche. They wore their pride like a shield. There could be no show of vulnerability.

When Michelle's husband Rob had fallen fatally ill, he'd been so adept at hiding his fears and emotions, he'd created a wall between them she could never breach.

"How come you aren't working?"

Lynette's truculent tone made the situation transparent to Michelle. Now that Zak was home for a while, her niece wanted to spend as much time with him as possible.

Since college he'd made several trips a month from Carlsbad to Riverside to visit the family, but he hadn't come nearly as often as Sherilyn and Graham would have liked.

Michelle hadn't seen him in two years because she'd been out of town on one nursing job or another during those times.

Caring for various patients in their own households had been her panacea to get on with her life after losing her husband to Lou Gehrig's disease. The last contact she'd had with Zak had been at Rob's funeral.

"I just finished a job in Murrieta."

She didn't add that her patient, Mike Francis, the prominent Californian pro golfer on the PGA circuit, now recovered from his severely broken leg because of a car accident, had asked her to fly to Australia with him for an invitational tournament next month.

Beneath the conventionally handsome golfer's arrogance lived a man with a great deal of charm who could make her laugh. On top of that, she'd never been to Australia. The thought of exploring a little of Queensland and the Great Barrier Reef sounded intriguing.

Although she'd applied for a passport in anticipation, Michelle was still trying to make up her mind whether she should go. She suspected he would always love his ex-wife, yet she knew he was trying to make a new beginning with Michelle.

In the course of being his nurse, she'd learned enough about him to know he wasn't a man who made a commitment lightly. If she didn't want a new beginning with him just as badly, then she had no business going away with him.

Neither of them needed more pain in their lives.

"As long as we're on the subject, how grouchy is our patient this morning?" she teased in the hope of putting Lynette in a better mood.

"He's still asleep and won't want to be disturbed."

Her niece was definitely warning her off. At some point this summer Lynette had left her girlhood behind.

"I'm up now," came a deep masculine voice sounding an octave lower than she'd ever heard it before. Surprised, Michelle wheeled around.

Her breath caught.

"Zak—"

His six-foot-two frame was braced in the doorway at the end of the hall. Alarmed to realize what an effort he was making to remain upright, she started toward him.

"I thought I heard you talking to Lynette," he said as she drew closer. "It's been a long time, Michelle."

She swallowed hard.

Suddenly she had the answer to her niece's drastic transformation.

The last two years had brought changes. Adult changes. Still and always seven years younger than Michelle, Zak Sadler was a grown man now in every sense of the word. His black hair and strong masculine features made him utterly fascinating.

The aloofness that had characterized him years ago had turned into a compelling sensuality that threw out a male challenge Michelle couldn't possibly ignore.

He wore the bottom half of a pair of gray sweats and nothing else, unless you counted the bandage wrapped around the ribs of his chest.

Zak was all hard-muscled male with a bronzed tan that came from working in the California sun. At twenty-eight, he was a man in his prime, the head of Sadler Construction Company in Carlsbad, a beach city close to two hours away from Riverside depending on the traffic.

He'd always worked construction and knew how to save his money. Refusing Graham's financial help, he'd put himself through college to earn his construction engineering degree. According to her brother and Sherilyn, he'd built up an enviable business by bringing many of his former co-workers together. Apparently it was thriving.

Michelle couldn't help but admire him for knowing what he wanted and going after it with single-minded determination.

But right now all she could think about was Zak's impact on her. She'd known him for years as Sherilyn's adopted brother, but she'd never thought of him in a physical way until now.

Struggling to keep her voice steady she said, "It's good to see you again, Zak, but you shouldn't be out of bed yet. I was bringing you some fresh ice bags."

"Just what the doctor ordered."

Something in his tone produced a quivery sensation in Michelle's stomach that made no sense at all.

"Why didn't you tell me?" Lynette had walked up

next to Michelle, her avid gaze fastened on Zak. "I could have gotten some for you."

He gave a negligent shrug of his broad shoulders, bringing more muscles into play. "I appreciate that, but I didn't know I was hurting again until I came awake a minute ago."

The whole time they'd been talking, his unsettling gaze had been narrowed on Michelle. Now it flicked to Lynette.

"Aren't you going to be late for school? With the high cost of tuition these days, you can't afford to miss class. That's no way to start your freshman year."

Michelle shivered because she already knew how Lynette would react to those remarks.

Her niece's complexion lost color before she shot Michelle a hostile glance. In the next instant she flung around and headed for the stairs without saying a word.

Zak started for the bed with difficulty.

"Weren't you a little hard on her?" Michelle asked, hating to have been caught in the cross fire.

"Not hard enough," came the cryptic reply. "If you'll play nurse for a while, I'll tell you a story."

Heat swamped her cheeks to realize she'd almost forgotten about his broken ribs. That was one of the reasons she was here, to provide medical assistance.

By the time she reached him, he'd managed to lie down on top of the queen-size bed. His eyes were closed, his breathing shallow. The long thick lashes lay against his burnished skin. As she drew closer she noticed beads of perspiration along his hair line and black winged brows.

The shadow on his hard jawline and above his compelling mouth reminded her he was a man who could use two shaves a day, though she didn't imagine he had the time or inclination for more than one. Either way, he was so incredibly good looking her mouth went dry.

Michelle averted her eyes, horrified to discover that she felt an attraction to Zak.

How was that possible?

She moaned deep down as Lynette's words came back to haunt her. *He's not really my uncle. There's no blood tie between us.*

To her consternation, *her* body broke out in perspiration.

She placed the ice bags against his left side where she knew several two-by-fours being hoisted at a construction site had broken free to deck him and fracture two vertebrae.

"Ah...that feels good," Zak murmured.

While she was bent over to listen to his heart and lungs with her stethoscope, an errant strand of silvery gold hair trailed against his hard-boned cheek. His eyes opened.

Through shuttered lids she felt their hazel depths absorb every feature of her face. He seemed to take his time studying her softly rounded chin, the lines of her pliant mouth. His gaze lingered on her finely arched brows and lashes which were darker than her hair.

"Still the same pansy-blue eyes though they're not drenched with pain anymore. I'm glad to see the worst of your sorrow has passed."

Shaken by his words, the intensity of gaze, she purposely flashed him her professional smile in an effort to conceal her awareness of him. "I'm much better these days, thank you."

After she'd finished taking his blood pressure, she

stood up and put her equipment away. "You're the one your sister's worried about. A collapsed lung is no joke. You shouldn't have gotten up without someone to assist you."

"I had my reasons." That was the second veiled reference to something bothering him.

She felt for his pulse. "And I have mine."

"Yes, Nurse," he teased.

In this mood Zak was...irresistible. She was fast losing all objectivity.

"You were struggling in the doorway just now. Your vital signs don't lie."

He let out a frustrated sigh. "You're right. I feel like hell. When do you think I'll be well enough to get back on the job?"

If only once Rob could have admitted to his misery in front of her like Zak had done just now, they could have shared so much. But he wasn't the kind of man to let go. His determination to suffer in silence had pushed her away, hurting her and he'd known it.

She let go of Zak's strong, suntanned arm, noting the cleanliness of his hands and nails. Despite working in construction, he'd always been well groomed. He always smelled good.

Don't do this, Michelle. What are you thinking?

"I'm not your doctor, but I'd say three to four weeks, barring no complications."

"I can't stay away from the condo any longer."

She leaned back against the dresser with her arms folded. "You don't have much choice. You need help."

"I agree."

His penetrating gaze followed the lines and rounded

curves of her slender body dressed in cream linen pants and a sage colored, short-sleeved blouse.

Her pulse raced in reaction. She was helpless to stop it, and that made her more nervous than ever.

"You've put on some weight since the last time I saw you, Michelle. It looks good." His husky tone sent a coil of warmth through her body. "Why don't you pull up a chair and sit down. I want to discuss something with you."

Zak hadn't said or done anything wrong, yet she felt like she was suffocating in the enforced intimacy of the bedroom with him lying there so close and so...

She'd thought the brief feeling of guilt she'd experienced at the funeral when she'd found herself comparing Zak's openness to Rob's inability to let her comfort him would be gone by now.

In the interim she'd begun dating again and had met some very attractive men. Mike Francis was a case in point. So why wasn't she thinking about Mike right now?

"Before I do that, can I bring you something else to eat? Some strawberry dessert maybe? It doesn't look as if you've touched your breakfast." The tray of food Sherilyn had brought up earlier still sat on the far side of the bed.

"The pills I'm taking have killed my appetite."

"Then you need some medication to get rid of the nausea."

"That's the least of my problems," his voice grated. "It's important I talk to you about something else before Sherilyn gets back."

Suddenly Michelle was transported to the past when

a much younger Zak had sought her out to confide something in private.

Anxious to appear at ease around him the way she once was, she complied with his wishes and drew the bamboo chair from the corner of the room.

"What's wrong?" she asked after subsiding into it.

His eyes were closed again, as if the mere act of talking was an effort for him. It probably was if he felt so sick to his stomach he couldn't eat. "It's about Lynette."

Hearing her niece's name reminded Michelle of the unpleasantness in the hall earlier. Without being aware of it, she rubbed her palms over her knees. "She wanted to stay home and help you."

He made a strange noise in his throat. "Three weeks ago she lied to her parents about sleeping over at Jennifer's and drove to Carlsbad to see me instead," he explained without acknowledging her remark.

"When I came home for lunch, I found her waiting in my condo dressed, or should I say undressed, in the kind of bikini Sherilyn would never approve of.

"She'd let herself in the back entrance with the key I gave them in case of an emergency. To say I was shocked is putting it mildly."

"I can imagine," Michelle whispered. "I'm afraid you've been the object of hero worship for a long time."

His lips twisted unpleasantly. "Throughout the summer she's been acting out in an attempt to flirt with me. But I never imagined she would go so far as to actually come on to me."

At that revelation, Michelle's breath caught.

"When I told her to get dressed and go home before

she was missed, she said Jennifer would provide an alibi for her. Then she walked over and threw her arms around my neck. After reminding me that we weren't really related, she asked me if I was glad to see her."

Michelle closed her eyes, unable to prevent the quiet gasp that escaped her throat.

"I as quickly removed her arms and told her I was due back to work any minute. After packing up the things she'd left strewn in my bedroom and bathroom, I forced her to give me the key.

"Then I walked her out to her car and told her to drive straight home. If I found out she wasn't there inside of two hours, I would phone her parents and tell them what she'd done."

After assimilating everything, Michelle said, "Did she do as you asked?"

"Yes."

"Under the circumstances, why did you let Sherilyn and Graham bring you here after you were released from Carlsbad Hospital? I understand there are several wom—"

"I need a qualified nurse like you," he cut in moodily, making no explanation about his personal life. "You'd know the kind of care I require."

She did. Since his chest tube had been removed, he needed to do regular deep breathing and coughing exercises.

"Sherilyn told me you're between jobs. That's why I came home with them, so I could ask for your professional help in person. I'd like to hire you to take care of me at the condo until I'm ready to go back to work."

What?

"I'll pay for anything the insurance doesn't cover.

There will be one perk at least. When you're not busy, you can enjoy the ocean. You've never been to my new condo.''

Her heart lurched.

''All you have to do is walk out of your own bedroom and step onto the beach. If you recall, it's perfect for swimming. How long has it been since you had fun playing in the surf or got a suntan?''

Shock almost forced Michelle out of the chair. It was with the greatest restraint she remained seated so he wouldn't guess at the true reason for the chaotic state of her emotions.

''The hospital stay has kept me away from my business too long as it is,'' he continued. ''It's vital I get back home where my assistant can come over and conference with me in my bedroom if he has to.

''With you there to supervise, Lynette won't be pulling any more stunts like the last one. Even if I could find another nurse, Lynette would find a way around her. I can't chance that.

''Let's pray to God some guy on campus will catch her eye and she'll be able to chalk this up to growing pains. The last thing I want to do is embarrass her, but I will if I have to.''

A shudder ran through Michelle's body. He never made idle threats. You always knew where you stood with Zak.

Lynette should have gotten his message loud and clear three weeks ago. The fact that she'd undoubtedly skipped class this morning in the hope of picking up where she'd left off with him, showed how in denial she was, how desperate she was for his attention.

"There's never been friction with the family," he confided. "I want things to stay that way."

"Of course." She rubbed her arms for want of something to do with all the explosive energy building inside of her.

"I told them in the car I was going to ask you to look after me at the condo. They seemed happy with the idea and urged me to talk to you."

"We're thrilled!" Sherilyn backed his statement as she breezed into the room. "No one will take better care of you than Michelle. An injury like yours is something she knows all about."

Michelle's head jerked in her sister-in-law's direction. She hadn't heard her in the doorway. If she'd come in the room a minute earlier...

Sherilyn, who'd bequeathed the same brown hair and eyes to her daughter, went around the other side of the bed to feel Zak's forehead. Her concerned gaze strayed to the tray. "Still not hungry?"

"H-he will be after I ask his doctor to prescribe some antinausea medicine for him," Michelle's voice faltered.

The second she'd spoken, she realized she'd committed herself to Zak. In the family's eyes there was no reason for her to turn down his request.

As for Zak, he needed her cooperation to quash Lynette's fantasies, among other things.

If by some chance Graham and Sherilyn were to find out what had happened at his condo three weeks ago and asked her about it, Michelle feared that in her niece's present frame of mind, she'd rebel in some way that could only hurt her in the end.

On the same note, it could turn ugly for everyone if she continued to harass Zak.

"I'm surprised the doctor didn't write something for nausea in the release orders," Michelle muttered absently. She couldn't force fluids if he was too nauseated.

When she looked over and saw the satisfied expression that had entered Zak's intelligent eyes, she started to feel afraid.

He could never find out she was attracted to him.

"Please tell me you two won't be leaving before tomorrow," Sherilyn pled. "Graham and I would like one more day to spoil the brother I hardly ever see."

"Don't worry," Michelle spoke before Zak could. "He's too weak to travel today. Also, Mike is taking me to dinner tonight."

Hoping the introduction of the other man's name into the conversation would somehow neutralize Zak's power over her, she leaped from the chair and pushed it aside.

"I'm going to bring you some ice chips and Coke. While I'm downstairs I'll phone Carlsbad Hospital and see if the doctor will do something about your nausea today. Hand me the tray will you, Sherilyn?"

Her sister-in-law gave it to her. "Ask Graham to drop by the pharmacy for the medicine. He's coming home early."

Michelle was glad her brother, a successful patent attorney, would be joining them soon. She needed space to sort out her emotions and get a grip on the situation.

The revelation about Lynette had been bad enough. By confiding in Michelle, Zak had made her party to certain private information which at this stage she agreed was better kept from Graham and Sherilyn. But

Lynette's infatuation wasn't going to go away overnight.

As for Michelle's awareness of Zak, that had to end
right now! On her way out the door she heard him say,
''Coke sounds good.''

She continued downstairs to the kitchen where she
phoned information for the hospital's number and made
the call. After being put on hold several times, she was
able to talk with the doctor who'd released Zak.

She explained she was the nurse hired to take of him.
They discussed Zak's therapy and his nausea. The doctor told her to have the pharmacist in Riverside phone
him on his cell, and he'd prescribe something.

Relieved for Zak's sake, she thanked him, then called
her brother who said he'd get in touch with their pharmacist and handle things from there. Once she'd given
him the doctor's phone number, she told him she'd see
him later.

With that taken care of, she went back upstairs carrying a tumbler of shaved ice and a cold can of Coke.
She found Sherilyn seated on the side of the bed talking
with Zak about his latest construction projects. His gaze
swerved to Michelle's and he stopped talking.

She approached the bed. ''Graham's on his way to
the pharmacy right now to pick up your medicine.''

''Thank heaven,'' Sherilyn exclaimed.

''Until he gets here, try alternating ice chips with sips
of Coke. Let me prop you first.'' Michelle put the things
on the side table before showing him how to grip her
arm and sit up using his feet and hips rather than his
torso for traction.

Since the age of twenty-two when she'd become a
registered nurse, and later after she'd gone on to spe-

cialize in orthopedics, she'd worked with dozens of male patients both in the hospital and later, after Rob's death, at her patients' homes.

She'd dealt with the broken bodies of old people, teens and athletes in the peak of physical condition. With one exception she'd never felt anything but professional concern for her patients' welfare.

In Mike's case, his determination to put their relationship on a personal level had won out.

Nursing Zak was something else again. She didn't know how long she could keep up a pretense of indifference when everything about him set off her latent hormones.

It wasn't just that he was a beautiful man according to the male order of beauty. After all, he'd been a very attractive teen. It was more than that. There was something in the way he moved, talked—his unique outlook on life—that aura of confidence and self assurance he'd always possessed—

All of it had combined to make him incredibly appealing to her and undoubtedly to any woman who knew him.

As if they had a will of their own, her eyes met his while he was drinking his Coke.

"You always did know what I needed," he said between swallows.

Michelle could scarcely breathe. The only thing to do was put distance between them.

"As long as Graham is on his way, and you've got your sister to help you, I'm going to leave for my house and come back for you in the morning. There's a lot I have to do."

She felt Zak's penetrating glance. "Don't forget your swimsuit."

While the blood was still pounding in her ears she heard a voice ask, "Where are you going?"

To her shock, her niece had come in the bedroom and Michelle hadn't even been aware of it.

Sherilyn stared in dismay at her daughter. "No hello first?"

Zak rested the can against his powerful thigh. His eyes still held Michelle's. "I'm taking Florence Nightingale home with me tomorrow. Technically speaking she'll be driving me, but it amounts to the same thing."

Michelle was aware that if Lynette could wish her to the other side of the ocean, she'd be there now.

Poor Lynette. No male students her age or any other could possibly compete with her uncle Zak.

"Michelle? When should I take his temperature again?"

Heat swamped her cheeks to realize Sherilyn had been asking her a question.

"This afternoon," she said. "Hopefully by then the fluids and medicine will have settled his stomach. If it's still elevated, give him some Ibuprofen. Get him up every hour to use the bathroom or walk around the room for a minute. I'll be by at nine a.m."

"In that case you'd better have an early night." Zak's unmistakable reference to her date with Mike reached her ears even though she'd disappeared from the bedroom.

CHAPTER TWO

"THANK you for dinner, Mike. I'd invite you in, but I still have some packing to do."

His arm was stretched out across the back of the seat. He toyed with the natural curl of her blond hair that curved beneath her jawline. To her chagrin she felt no accompanying shiver of excitement.

"That's all right. Carlsbad's close to my grandparents' beach house at San Clemente. Before we leave for Australia we'll have a lot of nights together after your brother-in-law has gone to sleep."

His words conjured an image of Zak lying on top of the bed this morning. Just remembering how he'd looked, how he'd made her feel, sent a flood of heat through her system.

Desperate for Mike to create that same kind of yearning inside her, she leaned toward him and pressed her mouth to his. It was the first time she'd taken the initiative in their relationship.

On a moan, he pulled her close and kissed her hungrily.

She should have expected this explosion of need on his part. They'd spent the last two months together while she'd helped him with his therapy. He was a normal male with normal desires.

She tried to get into it, but it seemed like the more she tried, the more it became the clinical experiment that it was. Before he started enjoying this too much, she pulled away guiltily.

"Good night, Mike. No—stay where you are."

He reached for her hand and kissed the palm. "I'll call you tomorrow." He looked too happy.

With a quick nod, she opened the door of his sports car and got out. It only took a second to reach the lighted front porch of the house. She waved to him before letting herself inside.

Long after the purr of the motor had faded, Michelle was still standing in the middle of the living room, immobilized.

She should never have kissed Mike like that.

He'd been very patient with her so far. She knew he was hoping they'd become intimate in Australia. After reaching out to him just now, he was counting on it. But the whole situation had backfired on her because she couldn't imagine kissing him again.

In truth, she couldn't bear the thought of him touching her. The chemistry wasn't there. It never would be. She knew that now.

Mike was a wonderful man. If he didn't reconcile with his ex-wife, then he deserved to find a woman he could set on fire by her just thinking about him. Michelle wasn't that person.

After her disturbing response to Zak who'd done absolutely nothing to make her come alive, she realized she couldn't go on giving Mike hope. It wouldn't be fair to him.

When he called her tomorrow, she would tell him Zak's injury was more serious than she'd realized. Her brother-in-law was going to need her help for an indefinite period, so she wouldn't be able to fly to Sydney with him after all.

The sooner Mike learned the truth, the sooner he could deal with his disappointment and move on. With a golf tournament coming up in a month, he needed to focus on his game.

Her gaze wandered around the room of the modest ranch style home where she and Rob had lived. It was here she'd nursed her husband until the last month when he'd had to be in the hospital.

After his death she'd liked getting away from it for weeks, even months at a time, then returning for a few days' rest before another job came along.

Now a new job *had* come along. One she couldn't have turned down without raising questions she couldn't answer.

But this was a job different from any she'd had before.

She buried her face in her hands. How was she going to handle living with Zak day and night for the next month and not give herself away?

Until this morning she'd thought maybe she'd never feel the desire for physical intimacy with anyone again.

But one minute in Zak's presence and she'd turned into a trembling mass of needs he'd ignited without even touching her or being aware of his effect on her.

She drew in a ragged breath.

Was it because Zak was so much younger than her husband or the men she'd been dating who were closer to forty, like Mike?

Rob had been thirty-seven to her thirty when she'd married him. They'd enjoyed a satisfying love life when he wasn't too exhausted from being up in the night with sick children. She'd tried to get pregnant but it hadn't happened.

After he fell ill, they mostly held each other. Some days and nights he felt good enough to make love, but those times grew less frequent as the disease took over.

Could it be she was one of those needy, over-the-hill widows whose senses only responded to the virility of youth anymore? She'd be thirty-six next March with a marriage already behind her.

Zak was a young and vigorous man still enjoying his single status until the right woman came along. A whole new world would open up to him when that happened.

Her feelings for Zak had always run deep because both of them had lost their parents in accidents. They'd had that loss in common and it had drawn them together. But it was shameful to be entertaining the thoughts she had about him now.

Though Lynette's infatuation was no doubt alarming as well as irritating to Zak considering they belonged to the same family, he could forgive it because a young woman's adoration was understandable. But if he could have known Michelle's reaction to him this morning, he'd be repulsed.

If Mike knew how Zak made her feel, he'd be so hurt!

That's why Michelle had to end it with him tomorrow.

After cleaning up the house, she got ready for bed. By the time her head hit the pillow, she'd worked out what she was going to say to him in the hope it would cause the least amount of pain.

But to her chagrin she wasn't any closer to a solution that would make her immune to Zak's powerful masculine appeal. All she could do was stay busy and mentally isolated from him when he didn't require her help. That meant she needed to find an engrossing project.

She knew Zak had a computer at his work and the condo. Sherilyn and Graham had confided that e-mail was the best way to stay in touch with her brother between visits.

If it wasn't too late, Michelle could use his to sign up for an on-line class through UCLA. Something challenging with a lot of homework, yet unrelated to her profession.

Relieved for that little bit of inspiration, she finally fell asleep. But it was fitful. She came awake before her alarm went off at seven.

After she'd showered and washed her hair, she dressed in blue denims and sandals. The rest of her outfit included a navy tank top layered with a white short sleeved, button-down blouse.

Yesterday afternoon she'd made arrangements about the house with the next door neighbor she paid to keep an eye on her place. Myrna Jensen had become a loyal friend who'd been so supportive of Michelle since Rob's passing and could use the money. Michelle could trust the other woman to forward on her mail to Zak's condo.

With that already accomplished, all she had to do this morning was pack.

And try to ignore this strange new sense of excitement she couldn't ever remember experiencing before.

Surely it was a transitory aberration brought on because Zak had always been one of her favorite people. She hadn't seen him for such a long time and he'd grown up a lot during the last two years.

That *had* to be the reason.

When she saw him again this morning, it wouldn't be like yesterday. Her heart wouldn't thud. She wouldn't feel that weakness in her limbs. She wouldn't concentrate on his mouth, imagining what it would feel like if it were covering hers.

Don't, Michelle. Just…don't.

She jerked a medium sized piece of luggage from the storage closet.

September at the beach could be warm to hot, or punctuated with days of fog and cooler weather, even rain. She'd better go prepared for any eventuality.

Michelle had become an expert at arranging things in one suitcase. As soon as she'd placed the cosmetic kit and medical case on top of her clothes, she closed the lid ready to go.

Remembering a time when Zak was recovering from an appendectomy and had enjoyed her reading to him, she pulled a couple of novels from the bookcase and put them in her purse along with her cell phone.

On the way out the door she grabbed the airline bag filled with crossword puzzles, board games, several decks of cards, a little battery operated radio, plenty of scratch paper and pens. Anything to help her patients escape the frustration of their physical inactivity. She never left for a job without it.

En route to Graham's house she made three stops. One to a drive-in for breakfast. She ate while she drove to the service station to gas up the three-year-old Audi and get her tires checked. Last but not least, she bought several sacks of groceries at the supermarket. A half hour later she reached her destination and pulled in the driveway.

Because of Zak's long legs, he'd be better off in a

semi-reclining position in the front seat while they drove to Carlsbad. She got out of the car and went around to the other side to push the seat back as far as it would go. After making a few adjustments, she hurried past the tubs of flowering azaleas to the front door and rang the bell.

Her brother, who was dark blond with a lean six foot build, greeted her with a hug. His soulful blue eyes stared into hers. "I have to tell you I'm relieved you're going to be the one looking after Zak. He puts on an act, but that's all it is."

"That chest tube was no fun, and he sustained a lot of bruising along with those fractured ribs. Give him a week and you'll see a big difference. Is he running a temperature this morning?"

"A slight one."

"That's probably because he's so anxious to get back to Carlsbad. How's the nausea?"

"Sherilyn managed to get him to eat some scrambled egg and toast. So far he's kept it down."

"Good. The medicine's helping then."

"Thanks to you."

She cocked her head. "Graham? Something else is wrong. What is it?" She was pretty sure she knew it had to do with Lynette, but she felt compelled to ask in order to be prepared for any eventuality.

He frowned. "Our daughter. Early this morning she came in our bedroom and announced she was withdrawing from her classes."

Oh no.

"It seems she's decided to find a full-time job. As soon as she's earned enough money, she plans to move to her own apartment. Before we could get a word in, she left the house and drove off.''

''I'm so sorry.''

''Zak's always been a strong influence. If he weren't incapacitated right now, I'd ask him to talk to her.''

Michelle's eyes closed tightly. His lecture to Lynette yesterday on top of his rejection of her three weeks ago had burned her deeply. Was he even aware of this latest crisis? If not, she would tell him about it on the way to Carlsbad.

''I'm afraid her mother and I aren't her favorite people right now,'' her brother murmured.

This was one time she couldn't comfort him. Not when she knew what was at the bottom of her niece's unprecedented behavior. It was the kind of situation only time could solve.

''It's obvious Lynette is trying to find herself. Maybe she *should* work for a while and find out what it's like in the cold cruel world. By spring semester she'll probably be eager to live at home again and get back in school with her friends.''

He raked a frustrated hand through his hair. ''I hope you're right.''

She put her arm around him. ''I know those words are cold comfort at the moment. Just give it some time. She knows she's got the greatest parents on earth.''

He gave her a brief smile. ''Thanks. That's nice to hear. By the way, how was your evening with Mike?''

''Good,'' she answered without blinking an eye.

''Don't let Zak give you a hard time about him.''

Her pulse quickened. ''What do you mean?''

''I believe he's as protective of you as I am.''

''Zak?'' she cried softly.

Graham nodded. "He's of the opinion Mike Francis is a womanizer. That's the polite version of what he told me last night."

"Zak should know the media sensationalizes everything. I've gotten to know the real Mike. He's a terrific person."

"I'm sure he is or you wouldn't be dating him. That's what I told Zak." He winked. "Just thought you'd like to know I'm on your side."

"I appreciate that."

How ironic that she'd already decided to stop seeing Mike, and all because of Zak.

His mere existence was causing turmoil in this house. Judging by the shadows beneath Sherilyn's eyes as she came down the stairs to find Graham, it wasn't over yet.

"Darling? Zak heard the bell and wondered why you haven't come up for him yet."

"I'm on my way." He kissed his wife's cheek before taking the stairs two at a time.

Michelle hurried over to her sister-in-law and gave her a hug. "He was telling me about Lynette."

"I can't believe what's happened." Tears entered her eyes. "If that's not bad enough, Zak's going away again. We see so little of him as it is."

"Why don't you come to the beach on Sunday, with or without Lynette. I'll fix dinner. We haven't all sat down together for a long time. It'll be good for everybody."

It'll be good for me to have family around.

"That makes me feel better already. I'll bring the dessert."

"Just bring yourselves. Let me wait on you for a change. In fact while I'm taking care of him, why don't you plan on coming every Saturday for the next month and staying overnight.''

''You'd have to check with Zak first. He keeps his private life to himself, but I know he has a girlfriend because she called his room every day while he was in the hospital.''

For some strange reason Michelle didn't want to hear about that. She didn't want to think about him being intimate with another woman.

Furious with herself because she shouldn't care about Zak's private life one way or the other she said, ''I guess we can talk about future plans on Sunday. Now tell me where his medications are.''

''In the kitchen. I'll get them.''

''Okay. I'll meet you at the car.''

Relieved she wouldn't have to have physical contact with Zak until they reached Carlsbad, Michelle hurried outside and opened the front passenger door.

The month wouldn't be nearly as difficult to get through if the family showed up on a regular basis. Maybe a miracle would happen and Lynette would come to her senses before this weekend was over.

Michelle slid behind the wheel and shut the door, ready to begin her nursing job. That's what it was. She had a patient to take care of. Period.

Out of the periphery she saw Zak walk slowly toward the car with her brother and sister-in-law bracing him on either side. This morning he was dressed in sandals and the same pair of gray sweats.

Her thoughts raced ahead. In a few minutes they were going to be alone. She sat there and waited, not daring to look at him.

No one could actually help Zak get in the car. The

breath he expelled when he lay back against the seat told her what the effort had cost him.

Graham set an overnight bag in the back seat, then shut both doors. "Drive safely."

Sherilyn nodded. "Two of our favorite people are inside."

"Michelle was always an excellent driver," Zak murmured. "For a number of reasons I couldn't be in better hands."

Zak's voice seemed to have taken on a velvety quality just then. She'd felt it resonate to the very core of her being.

Her hands tightened on the wheel. "I promise to call you when we get there so you'll stop worrying. See you on Sunday," she called to them before backing out of the driveway.

Once they drove off he drawled, "What's happening on Sunday?"

"They're coming for dinner."

"That sounds nice."

"I think so, too." She was pleased the thought of it made him happy.

"It'll be good for Lynette to see everyone together," he murmured.

His comment convinced her he didn't know the latest development. She waited until they reached the freeway to tell him what had happened earlier that morning.

"Your remarks to Graham were right on," Zak said when she'd finished relating the gist of the conversation with her brother. "Lynette's perspective will change once she's part of the working world. She's a smart girl. Given time she'll figure out her life."

"That's easy enough for both of us to say, but then she's not our daughter."

She bit her lip when she realized what she'd just said.

"If Lynette were ours, at least we know we'd be in agreement over our course of action. Speaking of children, I know you always wanted a family one day. Did Rob's illness affect your ability to conceive?"

Considering the fact that she and Zak used to be able to talk about anything, she shouldn't have been surprised by his personal question. But that was before this…awareness of him had sprung into existence with a life all its own.

She had no choice but to tough out moments like this if she was going to last as long as it took to take care of him.

"He became ill before I could make an appointment with my obstetrician to undergo tests for infertility. When Rob was diagnosed, he felt it best we didn't pursue trying to bring a child into the world."

She could still hear her husband saying those words in his quiet yet implacable tone that brooked no argument.

"I realize his opinion was colored by all the single mothers whose children he took care of in the emergency room. No father around, no husband providing for them. No hope for a happier future. He wanted me to be free to get on with my career, my life."

She heard Zak take a deep breath. "His reasoning makes perfect sense. In his place I would have said the same thing. To know you were going to die would bring out every protective instinct to leave your spouse in the best circumstances possible.

"But I'm not in his place yet, thank God, and I can

see how much comfort you would have derived from having his child to love and nurture.''

Don't say anymore, Zak. You understand too much. You have a wisdom beyond your years. You always did.

It was time to change the subject.

''Sherilyn told me there was a woman who called you at the hospital every day. I don't remember hearing her name.''

''It was probably Breda Neilson.''

That sounded Scandinavian. Most likely she was statuesque and beautiful.

''Why don't you ask her for dinner on Sunday?''

''Does this mean you've already invited Mike Francis?'' He'd fired the question at her so fast she was stunned. Graham had warned her.

''Of course not. When I'm on duty I don't mix business with pleasure.''

''Just after hours,'' came the baiting rejoinder.

''I'd rather not talk about Mike if you don't mind.''

''He's not the right man for you, Michelle.''

She'd already found that out on her own, but not for the same reasons Zak judged him. Maybe it was better he didn't know she was about to end it with Mike. For her own self-preservation the pretense of a love interest could help act as a buffer against Zak's devastating charisma.

She fought for a steadying breath. ''What I was trying to say is, you must know Graham and Sherilyn would love to meet anyone important to you.''

''When that day comes, they'll know all about it. How long was Mike Francis laid up with his broken leg?''

They were back to Mike again.

"After he was released from the hospital, two months."

"I understand his townhouse borders the golf course."

"Yes."

"To look out the window every day and know he couldn't work on his putting, which needs a lot of help by the way, must have been tough on him."

"It was."

"But not too tough with you there to see to his every need."

His innuendo sent warmth to her cheeks.

"Between therapy sessions he watched videos of his game to see where he could improve."

"Is *that* what he told you," came the mocking reply. "No doubt it fed his ego for you to sit for hours admiring him."

Michelle blinked. Zak really didn't like him. How could he possibly swallow all the lies fed by the media? Why did he care?

"Nursing Mike taught me about the game of golf. I never understood it or had an interest in it before."

"And now you do."

"Yes. Not to play, but to watch. It takes incredible skill and tenacity."

After a pause, "Did you know his wife left him because he'd had a string of affairs?"

Michelle might not be in love with Mike, but she cared enough about him to disabuse Zak of that myth.

"It's the other way around. He divorced his wife when he found out she'd had an affair. She wants him back. I know because she came to the townhouse several times to try to talk to him. When he refused to see her, she broke down and talked to me, hoping I would intervene.''

A strange sound escaped Zak's throat. ''The truth probably lies somewhere in-between both their explanations.''

She'd thought the same thing. ''I'm sure you're right.''

''Are you prepared to be the new focus of the press?'' he demanded. ''If you can't see the way they'll exploit the nurse turns lover scenario, I can.''

Michelle *had* thought about it. Zak's blunt way of putting things only underlined her own misgivings in that department. However if she'd been in love with Mike, she wouldn't have let fear of the intrusion of the press stop her from being with him.

''How's the nausea?'' she interjected on purpose. ''Would you like me to stop somewhere and get you a drink?''

''I can see I've touched a nerve,'' he murmured. ''The answer to both questions is, my stomach seems to have settled down and I don't require anything more than to be back in my own home with my favorite nurse.''

She smiled. ''Sounds like the name of an old radio show. And now folks, stay tuned to *My Favorite Nurse*. I'm old enough to qualify.''

He let out a chuckle that was quickly followed by a groan. ''Somebody lied,'' he said. ''It takes more muscles to laugh.''

''Except that laughter has other medicinal qualities to cure what ails you.''

''I happen to agree. Now tell me where in the hell you ever got the idea that you were old.''

"When you reach the venerable age of thirty-five, you won't have to ask that question. Fortunately for you, that time is many years away yet."

"If anyone were listening to us, they'd assume you were talking to a child. Don't you know once a person reaches adulthood, age becomes a relative thing? You're feeling old inside because you've been nursing patients nonstop since college."

This line of conversation was starting to make her uncomfortable.

"You didn't even take time off from your work after you got married," he persisted. "When your husband became ill, you nursed him with everything you had in you, then lost yourself in the care of other patients. It's time for a change, Michelle."

"You mean I should find another way to earn my living *after* you no longer require my services?" she teased to hide her increasing turmoil.

"I'm talking a complete break from any kind of work." He sounded so serious, she was astounded.

"I'd go mad from boredom."

"Good, if that's what it would take to shake you out of your octogenarian mind set."

She pressed on the accelerator. "Anything else you want to get off your chest before we reach the Coast Highway?"

"I've only scratched the surface, but the rest can keep for later. We've got weeks ahead of us."

The reminder that they'd be alone together for the next month sent tremors through her body. Michelle couldn't explain her own overpowering awareness of him unless it was the fact that he'd been in the background of her life since Graham had met Sherilyn.

Once he'd decided to marry her, he sold the family home he and Michelle had grown up in. Being a protective brother, he found another house with a separate apartment for Michelle so they could still remain close.

Having lost their parents in a tour bus crash while on vacation in Mexico, both of them had known the agony of loss and felt compassion for Zak whose early childhood had been traumatic for him, especially when he'd only had three years with his adoptive parents before they'd also been killed in a car accident.

Though Michelle had been a sophomore in high school at the time of Graham's marriage, she'd found time to spend with Zak and be his friend. To Sherilyn and Graham's delight, even when she'd started nursing school and had a day off, she'd drive him to the beach at Oceanside or Carlsbad where they'd surf.

He was a natural and picked it up in no time.

Sometimes she'd take other boys in the neighborhood his age with them, but he inevitably sought her company. It was no hardship. They got along as if they'd been friends in another life.

When she thought about it, they must have explored every beach city between Laguna and Del Mar. He'd always loved the ocean at Carlsbad the most.

It hadn't surprised her to learn he'd decided to settle there upon his graduation from college. However it took Graham and Sherilyn some getting used to because they were crazy about him and would have preferred he live in the same city.

Sherilyn Sadler had been a first-grade teacher in Riverside when she'd married Graham Robbins. After her parents' death, she'd sold their modest home and moved to an apartment with Zak who was six at the time. For the next three years she tried to be mother and father to her little brother.

The money didn't last long and she finally got a teaching job. Then she happened to meet Graham Robbins at a party of a mutual friend. They fell deeply in love and married. With the loss of both sets of parents, the two of them determined to give Zak and Michelle the best home they could.

But it was another difficult transition period for Zak who'd lost his ability to trust.

All this came out when as a teenager, Zak confided his innermost thoughts to Michelle on their many outings.

He was bewildered by confused memories of being shifted to different foster parents, and couldn't understand how his birthparents could have abandoned their own flesh and blood.

Neither could Michelle. All she could do was listen.

In the listening, a bond was formed.

It went deep.

Maybe deeper than she'd realized to have survived the last decade when she'd rarely seen him or talked to him. Zak had been busy establishing his career, and she'd immersed herself in nursing both before and after losing her pediatrician husband, Rob.

Whatever the explanation for the impact Zak had made on her yesterday morning, he was no longer that angry, hurt, yet remarkable teen trying to understand his life.

Over time, with the help of Sherilyn and Graham's love, he'd managed to heal to a great degree and was already making an impressive mark in the world.

Zak would never know how much Michelle respected

him. She knew several guys in their late twenties who'd never outgrown high school and still didn't have a thought for the future.

Right now she'd give anything for Zak's birthparents to see what kind of man he'd become in spite of his upbringing. But that kind of thinking didn't get you anywhere.

As Rob had said many times, and he'd seen it all in his ten years of practice before he became ill, "Thank God for the resilience of a child's spirit."

Zak had been endowed with that resilience.

"We're near the ocean now," the subject of her thoughts broke the silence. He'd come awake from his catnap.

"The beach has always been my favorite place, too. If I lived here, I'd feel like I was on a permanent vacation. That balmy air. There's nothing like it."

She could taste it, smell it. The fog hadn't burned off yet. Maybe it wouldn't, but it didn't matter.

Unbelievably, she hadn't seen the Pacific in almost four years. Not since she and Rob, who had just begun to show signs of his illness, had come with the family for a barbecue Zak had arranged. He'd been renting an apartment then, building a business from scratch.

Her world had changed so drastically since that time…

"Tell me where to go." She'd stopped at a light.

"Drive south for two blocks, then turn right and follow the road down to the end. You'll see a private alley on the left. My garage is number 2."

In a few minutes she'd found the alley in question. In reality it was a cul-de-sac.

Sherilyn had shown her photos of the condos Zak's

company had been hired to renovate several years ago before they were listed on the market. Twenty stacked beachfront apartments had been converted into ten privately owned luxury condos, finished in a white cubicle style reminiscent of the Mediterranean.

Zak's earnings on the project served as a down payment on one of the two ground floor condos, making his dream of living on the ocean come true. Already she could tell the pictures hadn't done justice to the reality.

She came to a stop in front of his garage.

"If you'll reach behind me and open my suitcase, you'll see the remote on top of my robe with my wallet," Zak murmured.

Like a fool, instead of getting out and walking around to the back door, she undid her seatbelt and turned to feel for his case with her right hand. Not quite able to undo the lock, she stretched a little more and finally accomplished her objective.

Once her hand closed over the remote, she brought it forward. But in the process her body brushed against his shoulder. The contact sent liquid fire through every particle of her being.

In that instant their eyes met.

Between black lashes, his resembled hot green coals.

Without permission her heart began to hammer. Her palms started to ache.

Before she lost complete control, she sat back in her seat and pressed the button on the remote. When the door lifted, she drove in next to his white truck with Sadler Construction printed on the side.

Her hands were still shaking when he took the remote

and pushed the button again. The garage door enclosed them.

"I've been looking forward to this for a long time, Michelle. Welcome to my home."

CHAPTER THREE

"THERE," Michelle said from behind Zak as she fit the eighteen-inch-deep plastic wrap around his chest. It ran underneath his arms to fasten in back with Velcro.

"Your bandages will stay perfectly dry. Now into the stall. Don't worry about your sweats. After I've washed your hair, step out of them and finish your shower. When you're through, slip on the new pair of pajamas Sherilyn packed for you. I've put the bottoms next to the towel on the rack right behind me."

The water was already running. It needed to be the right temperature so he wouldn't react and jar that area of his chest which was healing.

She opened the stall door and helped him to sit on the little stepladder she'd set in place. Though she was five feet six, there was no way she could wash his hair with him standing up.

When his head was thoroughly wet she shut off the water and poured shampoo on his crown. Then she began a vigorous massage of his scalp. His vibrant black hair swirled around her fingertips.

He made a deep sound of pleasure. "That feels so good I don't ever want you to stop."

Michelle grinned. She knew how good it felt. "You're going to be a new man when you get out. Now, before I turn on the water and leave you, I'm going to wash your underarms with shampoo. Don't lift your arms! Just let me slide my fingers beneath them like this.''

Another moan of pleasure escaped. ''That feels even better than getting my hair washed. Did you do these services for Mike?''

On cue her face went warm. ''I do whatever I can for all my patients.'' *But I've never had one like you, Zak Sadler.*

''No wonder you're in demand,'' he muttered. ''My kingdom for a nurse.''

Already she could tell his spirits were improving.

''I'm turning the water back on. Let me rinse your head and underarms, then I'll leave. However I won't go any farther than your bedroom in case you need help. Call to me when you're ready and I'll remove the plastic wrapper.''

Taking great care, she turned on the water and made sure all the suds were washed away before she left him alone.

Sherilyn had packed new sheets with his clothes. Quickly, while Zak was occupied, Michelle removed the other sheets and made up his king-size bed. No sooner had she finished putting new cases on the pillows than she heard him call out, ''Nurse!''

She chuckled. There would always be a little bit of a devil inside Zak. If it were a real call for help, he'd have cried her name.

''Coming!''

''What do you think?'' he asked when she opened the door.

What she thought, and what she said when she saw him standing there like an Adonis in black Ralph

Lauren designer pajamas riding low on his hips, were two different things.

"I think we need to do something about that wet hair." She moved behind him and undid the plastic wrapper, then she reached for a hand towel. "Come on. Let's seat you on the edge of the bed."

She supported his upper arm while they walked into the bedroom. Once he was sitting down, she gently dried his wavy hair which he wore fairly short cropped.

After combing it the way he liked it, she pronounced him ready to do his exercises.

He frowned. "And here I was thinking you were an angel from heaven."

"You want to get well faster, don't you?"

"That all depends now that you're here."

She wished he wouldn't say things like that. He was only teasing, while she—

Deal with yourself, Michelle.

Grabbing the nearest pillow, she placed it against his torso and had him lean forward to cough. Then she had him do his deep breathing exercise to fill his lungs to capacity so they'd function the way they did before his accident.

"I'm not having fun yet," he complained a few minutes later.

She told him to be quiet while she listened to his heart and lungs with the stethoscope.

"The good news is, everything sounds great in there. Now let's get you on the bed and settled against the pillows."

Once that was accomplished she had him take his medications. "Before I cover you with the sheet, I'll rub your hands, then your feet."

She squirted lotion in her palms and began her massage without looking at him. He was a man who worked with his hands. They were strong and callused. She smoothed several applications of lotion into the skin.

After she'd given his feet and calves a good rubdown, she told him to point his toes and rotate his ankles.

"That'll do for now." She pulled the sheet up to his waist and handed him the TV remote. "I'm going to make us lunch."

His hand grasped hers so she couldn't pull away without hurting him. Her astonished blue gaze flew to his.

"I've never been given this kind of care in my life. You were right. I do feel like a new man. Thank you." His voice throbbed with intensity.

Though she knew she should run away from him and keep running, she couldn't do that.

"It's been a long time since I was able to help someone in my sister-in-law's family." The deliberate mention of family was an attempt to get back on the easy footing of years ago, but it failed. She would never be indifferent to him as a man. It wasn't possible. "Would you like the curtains open so you can see the ocean?"

"Not right now." He slowly let go of her hand.

Maybe it was a trick of shadowy light, but his jaw seemed to have tautened. The medicine hadn't had time to dull the pain from the exertion of the shower and exercises.

"Your eyelids are drooping. Go to sleep. I'll be back with food in a little while."

Outside his bedroom she drank in gulps of air. It felt like she'd been running a marathon. If this was going to be her condition from now on, she had no idea how she was going to survive the rest of the day, let alone weeks.

There was no front door to Zak's spacious one level condo. You could enter through the back door next to the garage, or from the garage itself. Both entries opened into a rear foyer flanked by a laundry room and a storage room.

The central hallway led to the front of the condo. There were three bedrooms in the left half, two of which faced the water. A third one he'd made into a study that looked out on a flowering lanai hiding the next condo over.

A fabulous modern kitchen, dining room and step-down living room in honey-stained hardwood floors made up the other half of his condo. It was all open area so that no matter where you looked, you had a sweeping view of the ocean.

The interior colors were a mixture of cream and café au lait. Big puffy cushions on the sofas and chairs combined with pieces of rattan in a contemporary design made everything warm and livable. Paintings, greenery and flowering plants in pinks and oranges added contrasting splashes of color.

From the living room with its tiled fireplace, or from the front bedrooms, you could open sliding glass doors and walk out on a deep wooden deck decorated with huge pots of flowers that ran the entire width of his condo. A round umbrella table with chairs and loungers were placed at one end. A few steps down and you were on the beach. The continual pounding of the surf provided the final essential ingredient.

This was paradise.

That's what Michelle kept thinking as she made a

double recipe of beef and cheese enchiladas, one of his favorite foods. At least it used to be years ago. She prepared a tossed green salad with lots of avocado, and cut up some fresh fruit that included mangos and sweet pineapple.

In a week or so Zak would be able to eat out on the deck. Until then she would have to take him his meals.

Once she had everything ready, she added a can of cold cola to the tray and carried it to his bedroom which was decorated in the same colors as the rest of the interior with some brown accents for contrast.

He'd been in construction a long time. Because he worked with architects, it didn't surprise her he had such beautiful taste. As far as she was concerned, his condo was a showplace.

One of the coffee tables he'd made himself, Sherilyn had told her with pride. And now he was in the process of making a buffet for the dining room which he worked on after hours in the shop at his office.

"I didn't think I'd find you awake."

He'd been watching TV but shut it off when he saw her. "Now that I'm home, I'm hungry."

"That's always the way it is with my patients after they've been released from the hospital."

She placed the tray next to him, then helped him into a sitting position before handing him a plate and fork.

"Sit down and join me."

"I will in a minute, but there's something I have to do first." She pulled out her cell phone and called Sherilyn. Both she and Graham picked up on a different extension, relieved to hear they'd arrived in Carlsbad without incident. Zak's eyes never left her face while she was talking.

"Your brother is fine, Sherilyn. He's had his shower and done his exercises. Now he's eating lunch. I'll put him on."

Michelle handed him her cell phone. The conversation didn't last long. She heard him thank them for their help in and out of the hospital. Following that he told them he loved them and he'd see them on Sunday. "Here's Michelle."

She took the phone back. "Hello again."

"That had to be the shortest conversation on record," Sherilyn murmured. "Is he really all right?"

"I wouldn't lie to you," she assured them. "He's already devoured two enchiladas and is working on his third. Being back home is the best medicine there is. You know that."

"Thank you for everything you're doing," she cried with heartfelt gratitude.

"Amen to that," her brother chimed in.

"Hey—this is Michelle, remember? Helping Zak is pure pleasure. He and I used to be great buddies. Tell you what, I'll phone you tonight and give you another status report."

"We'll be waiting."

"Talk to you later."

She clicked off and reached for her plate, but something wasn't right. This was the second time since they'd arrived at the condo that she'd felt a strange tension emanating from Zak. She didn't think that brooding look stemmed from pain. His medicine would have started working by now.

"Has Lynette come home yet?"

With that salient question, Zak had solved the mystery for her. He was more upset about the situation than he'd let on earlier. So was she frankly.

Michelle put down her fork. "No, otherwise they would have told me. I sensed they wanted to talk about her, but were worried to discuss it knowing you could hear. They don't want anything to hinder your recovery and I don't blame them."

He'd finished eating everything on his plate, for which she was thankful. But before she could credit it, he'd put the empty dish aside and had reached for his cell phone. She'd laid it on the night stand when she'd unpacked his things.

A thrill of alarm shot through her body because she feared he was going to call them to discuss Lynette. If that was true, she didn't want to be in the room. This was something private between the three of them.

When she started to get off the bed, he put his hand on her arm. "I want you to stay and hear this."

He left her no choice but to remain seated. If she were to jerk away, she might hurt him.

"Hi, again. It's me," she heard him say in his deep voice. "Will you put Sherilyn on the phone as well so we can all talk? Michelle's right here with me."

As if the mention of her name reminded him he was still holding her arm, he finally released her.

She had a premonition of what was coming next and lowered her head. Zak didn't have a deceitful nature. Honesty was his trademark. If pushed, it could be brutal at times for the person on the receiving end.

Lynette's behavior had put him in an intolerable position. Now it was affecting the family.

"Good," she heard him say before he clicked off. When their eyes met he said, "Graham's going to turn this into a conference call, so answer your cell when it rings.''

With a sinking feeling in her chest, she clicked on her phone when it rang. ''Graham?''

''Hold on, Michelle, and I'll ring Zak.''

''I'm holding.''

Pretty soon both of them were on the line with her brother. There was a clicking noise. Sherilyn had joined them from another extension. ''I'm on.''

''Good. Go ahead, Zak,'' Graham urged in an anxious tone.

Michelle's heart sank because she knew they were worried there might be something else wrong with Zak. When they found out the real reason for this call, it was going to come as a shock.

''This is about Lynette. For some time I've been debating whether to tell you the truth. However in light of her threat to drop out of college and get a job, I'm breaking my silence because you deserve to know the facts so you can deal with the situation.''

Michelle froze.

They *did* deserve to know, but it took uncommon courage. Michelle could only imagine how hard this must be for Zak. She'd never admired him more than at this moment.

Without preamble, he told them everything except for the detail about the bikini.

''Blame doesn't enter into this,'' Zak continued. ''The fact is, I'm *not* related to the family by blood. Who can explain attraction? The shoe could be on the other foot. I could be the one attracted to Lynette, young as she is.

''In reality, she's ten years younger than I am and

I've always loved her as my niece. However if I were in love with her and she were older, I wouldn't let the fact that we're related through marriage prevent me from marrying her, *if* it came to that.''

Michelle gasped quietly. She'd known him to be blunt before, but what he'd just said had rendered her speechless.

''Now that you know all the facts, I'm hoping this will help you to help her.''

''You've just confirmed what we've suspected for a long time, Zak,'' Sherilyn spoke first. ''We love you more than we can say for coming to us with this news.''

''We do,'' Graham muttered. ''Frankly it's a relief to get to the bottom of her about-face. You're one in a million, Zak. You just keep going up in my estimation. I imagine you've suspected Lynette's interest has been more than hero worship, too, haven't you, Michelle?''

She gripped her phone tighter. ''Not until yesterday morning. Lynette was so upset to see me. After I reminded her she was going to be late for class, she told me she was capable of running her own life. That was my first clue.

''But I didn't have proof until I saw her pained expression when she heard I was going to be nursing Zak at his condo.''

''She'll get over this in time.'' Already Sherilyn sounded much more like her old confident self. Considering the delicacy of the issue involved, Michelle was stunned to discover her sister-in-law didn't find the revelation more than she could handle.

''With that off your chest, you can relax and concentrate on getting better, Zak.'' Graham seemed positively cheerful. ''We'll be there on Sunday.''

"We'll look forward to it."

After Zak hung up, Michelle clicked off in a daze. When she looked up, his gaze captured hers. "Mission accomplished."

The tension she'd felt radiating from him earlier seemed to have dissipated. She couldn't say the same for herself.

"My brother was right. You *are* one in a million. That conversation couldn't have been easy. Now you *do* need to rest."

Wary of being around him any longer, she got to her feet and picked up the tray. "I'll be back in an hour to get you up again. If you want anything else in the meantime, phone me on my cell. I've left the number on your nightstand."

"Your efficiency is without equal."

"Don't forget I was doing this job long before you got out of high school."

"I've forgotten nothing about you."

His comment shouldn't have haunted her all the way to the kitchen. Everything he said sounded personal, every look felt intimate. Yet in reality Zak was just being his normal self. It was Michelle who had the problem!

You're a pathetic older woman going through midlife crisis.

Disgusted and more than a little frightened by her vulnerability, she almost dropped one of the plates she was loading in the dishwasher. Once the kitchen was cleaned up, she wandered into the living room and opened the sliding door.

The roar of the surf seemed to match the painful pounding of her heart. She slipped off her sandals and ran down the steps of the deck to the beach which appeared deserted at the moment. There were only a couple of surfers riding the waves.

For the next little while she did a few deep breathing exercises of her own. The breeze flipped the collar of her shirt against her cheeks. She couldn't get enough of the intoxicating smell of the ocean while the foam swirled around her feet and ankles. It crackled and popped on the sand before rushing back to meet the next line of waves.

Zak swam here every day. This was his world.

He looked out on this breathtaking sight first thing in the morning, and all day and night too if he wanted. Heaven. Pure heaven.

It would be a wrench to tear herself away from here when it came time to leave. She couldn't bear to think about it.

Letting out a troubled sigh, she started retracing her steps back to the condo. Before she reached the deck she heard someone say, "Hi there!"

She looked to her right in time to see a well-honed guy of medium height with a marine cut jump down from the deck of the next condo over and hurry toward her wearing swimming trunks and a T-shirt. He looked to be about Zak's age.

"I'm Jerry Fowler from next door. I heard about Zak's accident. Is he out of the hospital now?"

"Yes. I'm his nurse, Michelle Howard."

He eyed her with male admiration. "How did he luck out like that?"

"I'm family." She hoped the added information would dampen his enthusiasm.

Instead, a smile broke the corners of his mouth. "Can I go in and say hi?"

She came to an instant decision. "I just brought him home, and am afraid the trip has tired him out. If you come by tomorrow afternoon about this time, I'm sure he'll be happy to see you."

"That's sounds like a plan. It was nice meeting you, Michelle. See you later."

He took off on a run while she hurried inside the condo. The hems of her denim jeans were still wet, but she'd shower and change after she'd taken care of Zak.

When she entered his room carrying two ice packs, she discovered him on the phone. He could be talking to anyone. Maybe it was his latest girlfriend, the one who'd phoned him in the hospital.

The second he saw Michelle, his searching gaze traveled from her windswept hair and down her body to her bare feet. It took her breath.

"My nurse is back to torture me some more." If Michelle weren't still trying to recover from the look he'd given her, she would have laughed at the comment. "I'll talk to you later, Doug." He clicked off and laid the phone on the nightstand. "Why didn't you put on a suit before you went wading?"

She placed the ice next to his phone. "I couldn't wait that long. Who's Doug?"

"The man I left in charge while I've been out of commission. He's coming over tomorrow."

"It looks like you're going to have two people dropping by. You'll have to be careful you don't get too tired out."

"Who else is coming?"

"Your neighbor, Jerry."

Zak's dark brows furrowed. "We're acquaintances by default. He's been living with his parents on and off since his divorce. I'll set him straight so you're not bothered by him again."

She was about to tell him she could take care of herself until she remembered something Graham had said.

I believe Zak's as protective of you as I am.

Deciding to let it pass she said, "It's time to get you up."

She pulled the covers past his feet so he wouldn't be encumbered. It pleased her to see he moved to the bathroom and back with a little more mobility. If he continued to make steady progress like this, he might not need her for a whole month.

It was close to five o'clock by the time she'd put him through his exercises. She gave him more medication and forced him to drink as much water as he could. Once he was in bed with ice packs in place against his ribs, she drew the covers to his chest.

"Would you like to watch the evening news?"

"Not unless you would."

Michelle could feel that fluttery sensation in her chest again. "Actually I was going to start your dinner." She'd said the first thing she could think of in order not to be alone with him.

"Aren't there any more enchiladas?"

"Of course, but I thought you might like—" She paused midsentence because her cell phone rang. She pulled it from her pocket. It was Mike.

"Aren't you going to answer it?" Zak's innocent tone didn't deceive her.

"That's all right. I'll return the call later."

"Feel free to talk to Mike Francis or anyone else you like in front of me."

And give Zak further opportunity to harass her?

Michelle shook her head. "You're my first priority. Since you don't want to watch TV, would you like me to read to you?"

His eyes gleamed with satisfaction. "I've been waiting for you to offer."

Her instinct about bringing some books along hadn't been wrong.

"How about *A Tale of Two Cities*?"

"I've read it."

"Ever heard of *The Screwtape Letters*?"

His white smile caused her heart to turn over. "No. I'm intrigued already."

"I'll get it from my bag. Just a minute."

The reprieve gave her enough time to phone Mike and tell him she'd call him after Zak had gone down for the night. She could tell he was frustrated, but he said he'd be waiting no matter how late.

He wasn't going to like what she had to tell him, but the hurt would be so much worse if she put it off another day.

After she'd returned to Zak's room, she settled on the side of the bed. "All my patients love this story. There's a head devil named Screwtape who sends letters to his nephew Wormwood on how to procure the soul of his earthly patient, a young man just trying to live out a normal everyday life.

"As you read each letter, you can see Wormwood's patient slipping from his grasp. So Screwtape's advice becomes firmer, yet gentler because he understands the workings of the human heart and its constant struggle between good and evil.

"This is C.S. Lewis at his best!" Michelle exclaimed, then she started reading.

It wasn't long before both of them were chuckling which produced coughing on his part, a beneficial by-product. As for Michelle, no matter how many times she'd read the story, it was like the first time. She loved it. She loved reading to Zak.

"How come you stopped?" He sounded totally disappointed when she put the book down after twenty minutes.

"Don't worry. I'm only going to remove the ice bags and put them back in the freezer."

She reached under the covers for them, pretending he was still a teenager down in bed after an appendectomy. But when her hands came in contact with his rock-solid physique, she was reminded he was an adult male who made her body grow weak even when she wasn't touching him.

"I won't be long."

"Hurry."

Her emotions were so chaotic she probably imagined the urgency in his plea. The book *was* engrossing.

When she put the bags in the freezer, she pulled out a cube of ice and ran it over her hot cheeks and neck to cool down. She hadn't even nursed Zak for a whole day and already *she* was feverish.

On her way to the bedroom she heard the doorbell. There was only one door. She walked to the back of the condo. Through the peephole she could see a woman standing there.

Michelle undid the deadbolt and opened it. "Hello. May I help you?"

"Hi. I'm Breda, Zak's neighbor upstairs. When I called his office, I found out he'd come home with a nurse, so I made some cookies and thought I'd bring them to him. Can I see him?"

Breda Neilson was a vivacious brunette who stood about five foot three, and was probably a good ten years younger than Michelle.

"I'm sure he'll love these. Please wait here a minute. I'll find out if he's up for company."

She took the paper plate of freshly baked chocolate chip cookies and carried them to Zak's room. His eyes looked from her to the gift she put on the side of the bed next to him.

"They're from Breda. She's at the back door. Shall I ask her to come into your room?"

Michelle couldn't read his enigmatic expression. "Thank her for the gift. Tell her I'll call her later."

Whether Zak wanted to see the other woman or not shouldn't have mattered either way. But the fact that he chose to put off seeing her brought a curious lift to Michelle's spirits.

"I'm sorry," she said when she returned to the entry. "Zak's tired out from his trip. He told me to thank you for the cookies and let you know he'll phone you later."

The disappointment on her face reminded Michelle of Lynette's expression when she found out Zak was going home to his condo with their aunt.

"How ill is he?"

"The worst is over. Now it's a case of his getting back his strength with physical therapy. In a month he'll be much more his old self."

Her eyes narrowed. "Will you have to be here the whole time?"

Breda was transparent, but then you would be if you were crazy about a man. Zak had that effect on women.

"It's up to his doctor."

"Okay," she muttered. "Thank you."

"You're welcome."

Michelle shut the door with the distinctly uncharitable thought that Breda Neilson wasn't the woman for Zak.

CHAPTER FOUR

IT WAS after 9:00 p.m. before Michelle left Zak and went out on the beach to make her call to Mike. The tide was coming in. She stayed far enough back from the water so it couldn't quite reach her.

"What did you just say?"

She bit her lip. "I can't go to Australia with you."

"I can handle that part," he murmured. "It's the other part I don't understand. What do you mean you've made the decision not to see me anymore?"

Michelle could hear his pain, but she decided she wasn't going to lie to him or make up some excuse about Zak's illness that wasn't true.

"It's for the best, Mike."

"Have you started believing the hype about me?" The hurt was there in his voice.

"Of course not. You know me better than that. The bottom line is, I'm not in love with you. Please—before you think this has anything to do with you, it doesn't! The problem lies with me.

"After losing my husband, maybe I'm afraid to let myself love again in the deepest sense. I don't know. I don't have answers. The important thing here is that you deserve to find love again. You're wasting your time with me."

"I can't believe what I'm hearing. What's changed after all this time? What was that kiss about?"

She groaned. This was so much harder than she'd thought it would be.

"Being away from you for the last week caused me to question how I really felt about you, about the wisdom of going to Australia. It started to alarm me. When we went out, I kissed you to reassure myself that my fears were groundless, but—"

"But there was no zing," he finished for her. "Is that what you're saying?"

"I-it wasn't just that, Mike."

"I agree. Something else is going on. You're like a different a person all of a sudden. Have you met someone else?"

She started to shiver and couldn't stop. "No. Of course not!"

"You sound too defensive. Be honest with me, Michelle. If we haven't got that, we haven't got anything."

He was right.

"Let's just say there's someone from my past I've seen again."

After a silence, "I thought we'd told each other everything."

"I *did* tell you everything," she blurted. "H-he doesn't know how I feel."

"You mean you've been in love with someone in secret all these years?"

"No. It was never like that!"

"Then how was it? Did you just discover you're in love with him?" Mike persisted.

"I don't honestly know what I'm feeling," she cried, struggling for breath. "In any case he's not in love with me. As for a relationship between us, it isn't possible."

"Is he married?"

"No, and that's all I'm prepared to say."

"Is he a priest?"

"No, Mike. You wanted honesty from me. I've said far more than I intended."

A long silence ensued. "There's something about this conversation that has me convinced your feelings run a lot deeper than even you know. I'd fight for you if I thought I had a chance, but in my gut I know I don't."

"I'm sorry, Mike," she said with tears in her voice.

"I am, too," came the tremulous response. "My life was starting to make sense again. Thank you for two wonderful months, Michelle. After the way you helped me, I'll always be in your debt. If ever you need a friend to talk to, and I think you might...I'm here."

"Thank you, Mike." He truly was a special man.

"You're welcome."

She heard the click.

Forgive me.

She put her cell phone away and walked along the beach where she passed half a dozen other people out enjoying the ocean.

Being honest with Mike had relieved her of a burden she hadn't realized she'd been carrying. Trying to make yourself fall in love with someone didn't work. It had to happen on its own.

Trying to fight an attraction didn't work either because it never went away. The only solution was to remove herself from the source of the temptation. Since that wasn't possible, maybe she should just stop worrying about it.

It wasn't as if anything was going to happen because

Zak aroused feelings in her. He was oblivious to her desires, so why the panic? She was overreacting.

In another week when he could move around more on his own, he wouldn't require her constant vigil. She'd made it through today performing the kind of intimate services she'd done for her husband, and she was still in one piece. She could do it again tomorrow.

That was the way to approach this. One day at a time.

With that much of a plan in mind, she returned to the condo and went to bed. Probably because she'd been honest with Mike, everything seemed better the next morning.

She put Zak through his routine minus the shower. When she started to give him his medication, he said he wanted to try going without the antinausea pill. That was a good sign his appetite had come back for good.

Soon after Zak had finished his second waffle and bacon, Doug Collins arrived with a flowering gardenia plant in one arm and a thick binder in the other. The cute brown-haired man with the dimples appeared to be in his early thirties.

"You have to be Michelle," he said the minute she opened the back door. "I've heard a lot about you. My wife Sandra and I let out a sigh of relief when we found out you were coming to take care of him. That accident terrified the hell out of everyone on the site."

Michelle felt a shudder rock her body to think he might have been hit in the head. Even wearing a hard hat, the impact could have killed him.

"The news terrified our family. It was awful. Come on through to his bedroom. He's starting to feel well enough to go crazy with inactivity."

Doug grinned. "I can imagine."

If anyone knew Zak well, she figured his assistant did. "You're the medicine he needs right now. I'll be interrupting every so often to get him up and put him through his breathing exercises. When you guys are ready to eat lunch, I'll bring it in."

"Sounds great."

Zak sat propped in bed reading a bunch of e-mails sent from his office he'd asked her to print out earlier that morning.

"Hey Zak—long time no see!" At the sound of Doug's voice, he lifted his dark handsome head. "Welcome back to the land of the living."

A slow smile broke the corner of Zak's mouth. Michelle looked away so she wouldn't feast her eyes on him. "It's good to see you, too, Doug."

"Sandra sent the plant with her love."

"Here." Michelle took it from his arms. "I'll place it on the dresser where Zak can see it and enjoy the fragrance. It's beautiful!"

"That's not all that's beautiful around here," Doug said, smiling at her. "Zak didn't exaggerate a thing about you."

"He put you up to saying that to keep the old lady happy."

Doug blinked. "Hey Zak— Have I missed something? Did you two get married while you were out of commission? If so, let me be the first to congratulate you."

Michelle knew her face had gone scarlet, but she had to brazen this out. "It was just a figure of speech, Doug."

"One she uses far too often," Zak inserted. "I'm

trying to wean her of the bad habit, but so far I haven't succeeded.''

Both men chuckled. When she heard Zak offer Doug a cookie, Michelle slipped out of the room. The latter's assumption that she and Zak had gotten married came as a jolt.

For the rest of the morning she did a wash and some vacuuming in-between Zak's therapy sessions. After she'd taken them a lunch of soup, sandwiches and iced tea, she made two apple pies for Sunday dinner.

While she was preparing a time-consuming recipe of butterflake rolls, Doug appeared in the kitchen midafternoon with their lunch tray.

"Something smells good out here."

She looked up from the dough she was forming into balls. "His sister and my brother are arriving tomorrow."

"So I hear. Zak couldn't be in better hands. Thanks for everything. When he's well enough to get out, Sandra and I want you two to come over for dinner."

Act natural, Michelle. Don't go all defensive or you really will give yourself away.

"That would be lovely."

"When you come, bring your iced tea recipe," he added. "I've never tasted anything like it before."

"Thanks."

"I'll let myself out."

"See you later, Doug."

She finished up the rolls, some plain, some cinnamon, and put them in the freezer, realizing it was time to take care of Zak again. But she dreaded it for fear he would talk about Doug's faulty assumption that they'd gotten married.

"How did the work session go?" she asked the minute she entered the bedroom.

He eyed her lazily. "We managed to wade through the bulk of material that needed immediate attention."

"Does that mean you won't be so anxious now?"

She didn't hear his answer because the doorbell rang. Lines darkened his striking features. "I don't want to see anyone else."

"It's probably your neighbor Jerry. He said he'd come by around this time today. I'll tell him you're too tired."

"No. Now that he's met you, he'll just keep coming over with an excuse so he can get you to go out with him." Zak didn't sound pleased. "Bring him in and stay with us. I'll get rid of him fast."

"It'll have to be fast because it's past time for your exercises."

On the way to the back door it occurred to Michelle that if she were attracted to his neighbor, she wouldn't like Zak's proprietorial manner with her.

But under the circumstances she had to admit she was glad of it. The man lived next door and could become a nuisance if he was always out on the beach waiting for her.

When Michelle answered the door, Jerry Fowler's bold appraisal left her feeling he could see beneath the sleeveless yellow blouse and white pants she was wearing. She hated that.

"Hi, again. How's the patient?"

"He's still worn out, but you can visit for a minute. Come in."

"It smells like Thanksgiving in here."

"I've been doing some cooking." She led him to the bedroom. "Zak? Your neighbor's here."

Zak had been pretending he was asleep. At the sound of her voice he opened his eyes. "Hi, Jerry. Michelle said you'd be over."

"How are you doing, Zak?"

"Not bad. How about you? Did that job offer come through in Fresno?"

"No. I'm still looking."

"It's been a rough time for Jerry, Michelle. He was recently divorced, and then his company closed down their plant. I hope things get better for you soon."

"Thanks. It looks like you're on the mend."

"With Michelle's help, I'm already feeling like a different person."

"Do you need your family's services around the clock?" He'd asked Zak the question, but he was looking at Michelle. "I was hoping you might like to go out one evening."

"Michelle and I aren't related by blood, Jerry, if you get my meaning."

While Michelle was still reeling from Zak's words, the other man said, "Whoa. Sorry I misunderstood the situation."

"That's quite all right."

"I saw Breda on the beach earlier today. I don't think she realizes what's going on, either."

"Breda and I have never been a couple, so no explanation is necessary. Why don't you ask her out?"

"Now that I know the facts, maybe I will."

"Thanks for coming by."

"Sure. See you around."

Michelle walked him to the door on shaky legs.

He paused on his way out, looking distinctly ill at ease. "Sorry if I trespassed."

"Don't worry about it."

After she'd shut the door, Michelle marched back to Zak's room. The satisfied expression on his good-looking face fueled her anger.

"When you told me you would get rid of him for me, I didn't expect you to say something that has given a totally wrong impression to everyone."

"Can you think of a better way to discourage two people neither of us ever cares if we see again?" he asked in a bland tone.

"No," she admitted honestly, "but I'm afraid you gave Doug the same impression."

"Don't worry about Doug. He knows the truth. How about reading me another chapter of Uncle Screwtape after you've put me through my paces? We were just getting to the good part last night when you told me I had to go to sleep."

There was no way to remain angry with Zak. He always managed to sound so sensible, you couldn't fight his logic.

Later that night when she'd settled him for the last time he said, "While I was in the hospital, I had my mail forwarded to the office. Doug brought it to me this morning. However now that I'm home, I've told the post office to deliver it here again.

"Starting Monday I'll ask you to get it from the box out in back. Sherilyn told me you'd be having your mail forwarded to my address, so no doubt it will be showing up any day. The key's on my key ring."

She nodded. "I was going to ask about that. Anything else I can do for you before I say good night?" He badly needed a shave, yet his dark shadow made him more dangerously attractive than ever.

"You could open the curtains and the sliding door and sit with me for a while in the dark while we watch the ocean together."

Her heart slammed into her ribs.

"Maybe for a few minutes."

She opened up the room to the ocean breeze, then turned out the lights.

"Come and stretch out so you can see without craning your neck."

It was a perfectly reasonable suggestion. If she did it without remonstration, he wouldn't guess at the turmoil going on inside of her.

Taking a few steps, she slipped out of her sandals and lay down on her side with her head at the foot of the bed, as far away from him as possible.

"It's about time you relaxed," came his deep voice out of the darkness.

The setting was so romantic she had to stifle a moan against her upper arm.

"The ocean's hypnotic, isn't it."

"Yes," she murmured.

"I never get tired of watching it. When I'm well enough, we'll take a midnight swim. That's one thing we didn't do together while I was growing up."

Talking about their past was too personal a subject for her to maintain an emotional distance.

"I'll probably be gone by the time your doctor gives you permission to get in the water."

"We'll see what he has to say at my appointment next Friday."

While she lay there hardly daring to breathe for fear

he would guess what his nearness was doing to her, she felt his fingers touch her ankle bracelet. A trickle of delight spread through her body.

"It's nice to know that on occasion you still wear this. I remember asking Sherilyn what she thought you'd like for your graduation from nursing school. She said women always loved jewelry. So, every day after class I did extra odd jobs at the construction site near the house to earn the money."

Her eyes widened in disbelief.

"The woman at the department store showed me earrings and necklaces, but nothing looked like you. When she could see she wasn't getting anywhere, she asked if the person I was buying the gift for had nice legs. I told her you had beautiful legs. When she showed me that gold ankle bracelet, that was it."

Michelle had assumed Sherilyn had bought the gift for fifteen-year-old Zak to give to her. "I didn't know the story behind the ankle bracelet, but I've always treasured it."

She couldn't take any more revelations tonight.

Sitting up quietly, she got to her feet. "You've had a big day today." She slipped on her sandals. "You're going to have an even bigger one tomorrow with the family coming. It's time for sleep." She locked the sliding door and drew the curtain.

"As long as you do the same thing."

"Good night, Zak."

She fled to the living room, knowing sleep wouldn't come for a long time, if at all. There was an oak hutch with doors that hid a TV set and entertainment center.

After turning to a channel showing old sitcom reruns,

she curled up on the couch in the vain hope they'd distract her from her torturous thoughts.

Zak's confession seemed to have set off a domino reaction inside of her. She started to reexamine every incident involving Zak since Graham had married Sherilyn. The comment about her legs didn't escape her.

It gave her a strange feeling to realize he'd been aware of her that way. He probably hadn't been any different than most fifteen-year-old boys who'd been noticing girls for a while.

But Zak had been her sister-in-law's brother, so she hadn't stopped to consider he might be looking at her as a woman. The rapport that made their friendship so strong had been the driving force in their relationship, or so she'd thought.

She undid the ankle bracelet and held it in the palm of her hand. Such a tiny trinket. Yet it represented thought and planning on Zak's part.

The woman at the store showed me earrings and necklaces, but nothing looked like you.

For him to make a statement like that meant he had to have studied her for some time to know her taste in things. What she wore.

Zak had a discerning eye for beauty in all forms. He took in the best of everything around him. His condo was a perfect example.

Was she making too much of what she'd learned? Probably so, but she found it odd, if not significant, that Zak would suddenly bring it up after all these years.

She'd worn the bracelet hundreds of times since her graduation. He couldn't have helped but see it around her ankle on various occasions. If he'd never been inclined to tell her the story behind it before, why now?

He never did anything without a reason. Zak was the most mature, focused, self-disciplined, on track individual she'd ever known. That was part of his fascination.

There were so many parts to his makeup. Complex parts. He could be inscrutable one minute, fun loving the next. Every second she spent with him was a challenge.

Frightened by the direction of her thoughts which seemed to be forming a spiral with Zak at the center, she jumped up from the couch and turned off the TV.

Morning would be here before she knew it. She had to try to get to sleep. Maybe she'd do better if she actually got in bed and huddled under the covers.

But no matter what she did, there were reminders of Zak everywhere. She was lying in a queen-size bed he'd bought. These were his sheets and quilts. His towels hung in the guest bathroom. Everything he possessed came as the result of his industry and remarkable talents.

Oh, Zak. Her body quaked beneath the covers. What was she going to do about him?

At some point oblivion must have taken over because the next thing she knew, the alarm on her watch went off. Seven o'clock. Time to get up.

She showered and washed her hair. After she'd dried it with the blowdryer, she applied a dusky pink frost lipstick.

During her week off, she'd bought a few outfits to replenish her wardrobe. One of them was a pair of straight-leg pants in an oatmeal twill and a tapered three-quarter sleeved shirt in pale blue. She dressed in the new clothes and headed for the kitchen.

They'd be eating at noon, so the pork roast needed

to go in the oven. She went over to the freezer and set out the tins for the rolls to rise. With that much accomplished, she headed for her patient's room.

"Zak—" she cried when she discovered him coming out of the bathroom. "Why didn't you call me if you needed to get up?"

He stood there without bracing himself against the door. She noticed he was freshly shaven.

"For the first time since the accident, I didn't feel the need for help. Your strict routine has already made me stronger."

"I'm glad to hear it. Nevertheless you've done more than you should. I'll help you get back in bed. It doesn't take as many stomach muscles to slide off as to climb back on."

"Is that so," he mocked her gently.

"Please don't start thinking you can do whatever you want yet." Her blue eyes implored him. "I don't want you to have a relapse."

"When you beg me so nicely, how can I refuse? I'm all yours."

One way or another he was going to drive her mad before she left to take another nursing job.

She assisted him on to the bed where he did his exercises. When he was through, she helped prop him against the pillows.

"There." She pulled up his covers. "Now for your pills."

"I can tell I'm not in as much pain anymore. How about skipping them?"

"Do me a favor and take your same dose today. If tomorrow you feel you can get along with less, I'll call your doctor and ask if it's all right to cut down."

"I guess I can't argue with that."

"Good. I'll bring you some breakfast. Does an omelet sound appealing?"

"Everything you cook is delicious."

"Thank you."

"Michelle?"

"Yes?"

"How come you won't look at me?"

Her eyes darted to his in surprise.

"That's better. Come closer."

She did as he asked, but she was afraid he'd see the pulse hammering away in her throat.

"Did I miss any spots while I was shaving?"

Her gaze wandered over the lower half of his face. With the kind of rugged chin and jawline that screamed "male," it took an effort of willpower not to reach out and explore every inch with her hands and mouth.

"No." By some miracle there was no tremor in her voice "You got everything."

"Come closer."

She couldn't breathe. "I promise you look fi—"

But the rest was muffled because he brushed his lips against hers. The whole experience only lasted a moment, yet it shook the foundation out from under her.

"Thank you for the care you're giving me," he whispered "I'm a lucky man."

Before she turned away she said, "I'm glad you feel that way. I'll bring your breakfast."

He'd caught her so totally off guard, she had to get out of the room. A second longer and there would have been no way to pretend the brief contact hadn't affected her.

Over the years they'd kissed each others' cheeks coming and going.

This was different.

This time Zak had crossed a line.

Was it because he'd sensed that his sister-in-law had wanted him to kiss her? Had she given off certain sensual signs only a man would recognize?

Were her eyes mirrors of her soul? Of their own volition had they blazed with desire for him until he'd decided to take pity on her?

Maybe that was why he'd told her the story behind the ankle bracelet. Why not give her a little thrill here and there to brighten her time on the job.

If that were true, all she could do was proceed as if nothing had happened. By the time he'd tired of his game because he was bored, she'd be off on another nursing job.

"How soon are we expecting the family?" Zak asked when she came in a few minutes later with a tray and the Sunday newspaper she'd found at the back door. She set everything down next to him.

"We're eating at twelve, so I suspect they'll arrive around eleven or so."

Without asking his permission, she walked over to the curtain and opened it. Like most mornings at the beach, the fog hadn't dissipated yet. She slid the glass door back, but left the screen in place.

Though he was lying back against the pillows, she could feel his eyes following her. "Where are you going?"

"To bring in the dining room chairs."

She made two trips. After placing them at the side of

the bed where he slept, she started for the door. "If you need anything, ring me in the kitchen."

"Before you get too busy in there, would you mind if I dictated a short note that I'd like delivered today? I'm so comfortable lying down, I don't want to move. You'll find paper and envelopes in the top right drawer of the desk in my study."

"Just a minute."

She returned with the items in question including a pen. "Go ahead," she said after placing the paper on the dresser.

"Dear Breda," he began. *"You and your dad are great neighbors. I found that out in the hospital when you showed so much concern for me. Thanks for going to the trouble of making cookies. After hospital food, they tasted delicious. The guy who wins you one day will be fortunate."*

"That's it. Just sign it, Zak. On the envelope put, *To Breda and Arnie.*

"When you find a moment, use the stairs to the left of the garage. They live in the condo above mine. Tape it to the door. You'll find some in the kitchen drawer next to the fridge."

It was the perfect rejection note. Very nice, yet like Lynette's experience, it would bring an end to the fantasy.

What Michelle had done to Mike had been so much worse.

"I'll take it up when I've got the vegetables cooking."

Michelle was out the door before he could say anything else. A half hour later, she climbed the flight of stairs to the second level. It only took a second to stick the envelope to the Neilsons' back door.

Relieved not to have run into Breda, she quickly retraced her steps. To her surprise she discovered some people walking toward Zak's back door.

They were a handsome Tongan couple with two children about five and seven. The way they were all dressed up, it looked like they'd come from church.

"Hello," she greeted them. "Obviously you're here to see Zak. I'm his nurse, Michelle."

The man gave her a sunny smile. "I know who you are already. I'm Miki Mokofisi, one of Zak's foremen. This is my wife, Melee, and our two boys Selu and Amato." All of them were holding a grocery bag of something that smelled delicious.

"We heard he had to stay in bed, so we brought him food," his wife said in a deep, melodious voice.

Michelle was touched by all the people who cared about Zak. "That's so nice of you. He's going to be thrilled when he finds out you're here." She unlocked the door. "Follow me through to the kitchen."

When they'd put their sacks on the counter, Miki said, "Looks like you're already taking good care of him."

"I'm trying. We're expecting family for dinner in a few minutes. Come on. You can surprise him."

"Miki—" She heard the warmth in Zak's voice when his visitors filed in the bedroom.

"Hey, Zak—with Michelle here looking after you, you're going to come back to work fat like me."

Miki wasn't fat. He was just big.

Everyone laughed, especially Zak who ended up

coughing, but he didn't struggle for breath. He really was improving.

"They brought you a homecooked meal," Michelle explained.

Zak smiled at the other woman. "You're a sweetheart, Melee. Do you think you and your family could come over for dinner tomorrow night and we'll eat it together?"

"Please do," Michelle urged. "I'll put everything in the refrigerator so it will keep. Come as soon as you get off work, Miki. Then your boys can swim before we sit down to a feast."

"That's exactly what it will be," Zak declared. "My mouth's watering already."

Melee's smile confirmed she was pleased.

Miki looked hesitant. "If you're sure you're up to it, Zak."

"What do you think, Nurse?"

"I think that if you rest all day tomorrow, the company of your good friends will be just what the doctor ordered."

Zak turned to Miki. "Did you hear that? It's settled."

"Whatever you say." The other man grinned.

"Yippee!" the children cried with excitement. They were so cute and so well behaved Michelle gave each of them a hug. "I saw some boogie boards in the storage room you can use."

"Will you swim with us?"

"You bet."

"Michelle's a good surfer, boys." This from Zak.

"Not anymore. I'm too old."

"Too old?" Melee put her hands on her hips.

"You're not as old as me and I won't be twenty-seven until my next birthday!"

At that comment Michelle felt a pair of hazel eyes impale her.

"*Yoohoo—*" a familiar male voice called out, "Anybody home?"

"Excuse me for a moment."

While Zak chatted with his foreman, Michelle hurried to the other part of the house. She found her brother and sister-in-law in the kitchen. They'd brought homemade fudge.

She glanced at Sherilyn. "Where's Lynette?"

"At Trisha's."

"Is she still determined to follow through with her plans?"

"Yes, but it's fine."

Her brother gave her a hug. "You know the old saying. The truth will make you free. Right now I'm more concerned about Zak. How's he really doing?"

"From a medical point of view, I'd say he's a good week ahead of where I'd thought he'd be by today."

Sherilyn's eyes lit up. "That's because of *you.*"

Michelle shook her head. "It's because he has an amazing constitution."

Her brother smiled. "I imagine it's a combination of both."

"Go see him while I finish dinner. He's got company, but they're on the verge of leaving."

Now that the family had arrived, she would have temporary respite from shocking things that kept happening when she found herself alone with Zak.

CHAPTER FIVE

LATE Tuesday afternoon, Michelle checked the mailbox and discovered a bundle of magazines and letters for Zak bound by a rubber band. There was nothing for her yet.

She went through to his bedroom and laid it on the bed next to him. He was still on the phone with Doug who'd called during different portions of the day to discuss business.

Because of the family's visit on Sunday, and the dinner with Miki's family last evening, she'd stayed so busy cleaning and acting as hostess, there'd been no extra time to devote to Zak beyond the nursing he required.

Consequently there'd been few moments where he'd been able to do something to increase her awareness of him, leaving her tied her up in emotional knots.

For that very reason she could wish they were looking forward to visitors this evening. Night was coming on and she halfway dreaded it because they'd be alone.

Starting to grow restless, she took the broom from the storage closet and went out to give the deck a thorough sweeping. When you lived right on the beach, it was so easy to track sand in and out.

The flowers in the tubs didn't require much care. They thrived on the humidity, but she still gave them a little drink of water before she went back inside to warm up leftovers for dinner.

A few minutes later she carried the tray to his room and set it down next to him. He'd moved all the opened mail to the other side of the bed.

Though she made a conscious effort not to look at him directly, she could feel him watching her. It was almost as if he were a stealthy jungle predator who'd been lying in wait, ready to resume his game of toying with her emotions.

"Since I've already eaten, you go ahead while I get something from my bedroom." She had a game of her own in mind.

When she returned, she carried Jeopardy under her arm. "I'm curious to find out if the accident has taken the edge off that keen mind of yours. The doctor's going to want a full report. You can participate without having to do more than turn a little card over in your hand."

He stared at her through veiled eyes. "I'll be happy to play if we do it my way."

"You mean because I'm well acquainted with this game, I have to get *all* the answers right."

"I'll give you a break," he drawled. "You can miss two out of the whole game against my three misses from each category. The winner gets to decide what we do next."

Michelle wasn't worried about losing. She knew a good ninety percent of the answers. Zak would have to concede defeat after one round.

"Agreed."

He continued to eat while they plied each other with questions. To her shock he didn't miss any on the History round. Neither did she.

Famous Author Pen Names came up next. "Who was Jean Baptiste Poquelin?"

She knew this! Unfortunately the answer wouldn't come.

His lips twitched. "One down for you and none down for me."

The race was on.

Next came the Geography category. They both continued to give right answers. Then came the last question. "The Seychelles are located near what continent?"

Again Michelle's mind went blank.

By now Zak's mouth was curved at one corner. "Two down for you. None down for me. A new category please."

"Astronomy." She was confident he wouldn't know the answer to the first question. "Define Star Grazer."

"A meteor that orbits the earth."

She blinked.

"Name the fifth planet," he fired.

"Jupiter."

"Give me another name for the North Star." None of her patients ever knew this one.

"Polaris."

He didn't miss a beat! Something was going on. No one got this many right.

"A concave mirror is part of what kind of telescope?"

"Refracting—" The second she said it, she knew it was wrong. Their eyes met. His were dancing. When he looked at her like that, she felt like she was falling through space toward him.

"You lose."

"What have you got under those covers?" she demanded in a cross tone. "Zak Sadler's special cheat sheet?"

"I have nothing to hide," he said suavely. "You're welcome to do a thorough search."

Heat scorched her face. She'd set herself up for that one.

His chuckle worked its way to her insides. "You can tell the doctor I passed the mental acuity test with a perfect score. You should be happy. It's your nursing skills that have kept me razor sharp."

"Okay, okay. I give up. What's your con?"

"We play it on the computer at my office during lunch."

"Oh, brother."

"You can't say I didn't win fair and square."

"No." She gathered up the cards and put them back in the box. "I can't say that."

He bit into a piece of fudge. "For our next game we'll play Guess What It Is?"

"I haven't heard of that one."

Michelle was enjoying this too much and he knew it! She'd indulge him for one round, then her patient had to go down for the night.

"You must close yours eyes, then you're handed something. You only get one guess, but you can take as long as you want before you give your answer."

"What if it's wrong?"

"Then you're given a clue."

"How many clues do you get?"

"As many as it takes to get it right. But you lose a point every time you need a clue. The person with the least amount of points is the winner. They'll decide the prize. Since I won the last game, I'll let you go first."

She had a feeling she was going to be sorry. Zak was a man, which meant he didn't play fair. But he seemed to be having a good time. Part of her job was to help keep up his spirits while he was on bed rest.

"Shut those gorgeous blue peepers and put out your hands."

With those words he'd transformed the tenor of the moment to the personal again. Damn him. "I'm ready."

What he placed there felt like a little book. She brailled the edges, then turned the pages. There weren't very many of them. They were made of a heavier material than ordinary paper. The booklet was solid.

When she ran her thumbs over the pages she could tell there was something embossed on each one. Inside the cover she felt something smooth, like plastic. She put the booklet to her nose. It smelled new.

"I think it's a bank book, or a savings book of some kind."

"Sorry."

He wasn't sorry at all. She could tell by the way he'd said it that he was smiling.

"Hmm."

"It's blue."

"Blue... That doesn't help me."

"It's something you don't want to lose."

"Is it an address book with important names and phone numbers?"

"No. You need it to travel out of the country."

Oh— Of course. "A passport."

"That's right."

She opened her eyes to look at it. "I didn't know you had one."

"I don't. This one's yours."

Confused, she opened the cover and saw the picture of herself she'd sent in with her passport application.

Her gaze flew to his. "I don't understand."

"It came in the mail today. I assumed everything in the bundle was mine and ripped the envelope open before I realized what I'd done. It wasn't intentional."

"I'm sure it wasn't. My neighbor must have forwarded it here. It came so fast! Trust you to think up an original way to give it to me."

She slid off the bed, clutching the passport in her hand. When she'd applied for it, she never dreamed how different her circumstances would be by the time it had been mailed to her.

"I'm going to put this in my purse so it won't get lost. When I come back, we'll do your exercises so you can get ready for bed."

"What's the hurry?"

The tension was back, throbbing and heavy.

"You need your beauty sleep," she quipped in a radical attempt to lighten the atmosphere between them.

Lines darkened his face. "I heard on the news Mike Francis is going to be one of the golfers at the Sydney Invitational in October. You're going with him, aren't you."

She took a steadying breath. "You know something, Zak? When you asked me if I would be your nurse, I agreed because I knew both of us were adults and would respect each other's privacy.

"I would never question you about the women in your life, or make judgements about the suitability of this or that person when it's none of my business." Of course that was a lie. Michelle hadn't liked Breda Neilson right off. "Likewise, I expect the same courtesy from you."

A bleak look entered his eyes. "Whatever happened

to the warm, open hearted woman who used to talk to me about anything years ago? Where has she gone? I don't know the person who inhabits her body anymore. I thought I did…''

His words might have been a knife plunged in her heart. ''That was unkind, especially consi—''

''Considering the fact that Nurse Howard has been waiting on me day and night?'' he cut her off with asperity. ''There's a difference between going through the motions of living, and actually embracing life. Like an imploding star, the Michelle I once knew has closed up until I can't find her.''

She winced. ''Is that what you've been trying to do since I came to work for you? Find me?'' Her voice sounded too shrill for her own ears, but she'd lost control of this conversation.

''In a manner of speaking, yes. Do you realize you haven't once asked me about my life? My associations? How I fill my time? What's important to me? My mistakes? My failures?

''The Michelle of my past would have been eager to catch up, to share what we've missed over the last ten years. Your husband died, but you never talk about it to anyone. Now you run from job to job with all your private thoughts and agonies locked inside of you.''

''That's enough, Zak.''

''You help others, but who helps you? Sleeping with Mike Francis isn't the answer.''

''How dare you!'' Her body was trembling so hard she thought her legs were going to give way.

''His top priority is golf,'' Zak went on as if she hadn't spoken. ''He can't stop Father Time who's his biggest enemy. When he goes to bed at night, his greatest worry is how he's going to stay on top of his game.

"His first wife found that out. No woman in his life can compete for his love when he needs to win another green jacket to validate his existence. You might travel to Australia with him, but you'll always be on the sidelines of his consciousness.

"It won't be long before he's part of the PGA Senior Tour. He'll never have the time to give you what you deserve. He'll never fulfill your dream to have children because he's following his own dream, and that will always be more important."

She gritted her teeth. "That's not my dream."

"Tell that lie to anyone but me."

Her eyes smarted. "Father Time has been my enemy too," she whispered in pain.

"Then do something about it instead of allowing yourself to be Mike Francis's comfort when he's in the mood for a little distraction."

"I already have," she confessed before she realized she'd spoken.

"What do you mean?" Zak jerked to a sitting position. He shouldn't have done that yet while his body was still healing!

She rubbed her aching temples. "I broke it off with him the other night."

"Thank God," he muttered.

"Not for any of your reasons!"

After a pause, "What other reasons could there be?"

"I-I'm not in love with him."

"You mean the way you were with Rob."

"With Rob it—" She caught herself before she went to a place she'd promised herself never to go. "The point is, though there's an element of truth in everything you said about Mike, none of it would stop me from being with him if my deepest emotions were involved.''

"So when did this happen? Did he show up at the condo after I was asleep?''

"No. This is your home. I wouldn't have asked him to come here. When he phoned, I told him I couldn't go to Australia with him. He knows it's because I'm not in love with him.''

"And he accepted that without a fight?'' Zak bit out. "He didn't tell you the tournament wasn't as important as your relationship, that he wasn't going anywhere without you?''

It should have been a wound to Michelle's pride that Mike didn't come after her and try to change her mind. In truth, she hadn't given him a single thought since she'd hung up the phone. But that was privileged information Zak could never know about.

"Mike must have heard the finality in my voice.''

"Finality be damned!'' His expression looked like thunder. "If you love someone, you do whatever it takes.''

That's *you*, Zak. But very few people in this world are like you...

She cleared her throat. "Mike's childhood was very different from yours. He was raised by affluent parents who still love each other. They've always loved him and have been there to support him and their other children.

"When he discovered his gift for golf, he was able to indulge it from an early age. His childhood wasn't plagued by financial struggle or emotional turmoil.

"He's not a fighter like you who became a self-made

man through sheer grit and determination. Maybe that's why he'll never be the world's number one golfer.

"I've spent enough time with him to know he's not happy deep down the way you are," Michelle admitted. "That's your gift. That's why everyone loves to be around you."

He studied her for a long time. "If that's true, then your absence from my life for such a long time, not to mention the fact that we've had no physical contact or even spoken to each other for two years, is more of a mystery than ever."

She sucked in her breath. "If you'd lost a wife, you'd have immersed yourself in work, too."

"To the exclusion of never getting together with the family? I don't think so."

"That's not fair. I've seen them between jobs. You don't leave your patients."

"Except that since the funeral you've always accepted jobs that took you out of town." His eyes flashed. "Somehow your in-between times never dovetailed with my visits, or family visits to my home. How do you explain that?"

She shrugged, trying to appear nonchalant when in reality this line of questioning had her jumping out of her skin.

"I can't. It's just the way things happened. I'm here now taking care of you, aren't I?"

"Yes," he murmured in a husky tone. "I couldn't ask for more than that."

Michelle averted her eyes. "Depending on what your doctor says at your next appointment, you'll probably be able to resume a more normal life around here. If there are times when you'd like the condo to yourself to entertain guests, all you have to do is tell me.''

''Why not just come right out and ask me if I'd like one of my girlfriends to stay over.''

The edges of the passport were digging into her hand. ''All right. Would you?''

''No.''

Michelle hated herself for the euphoria his simple answer produced.

''The last woman I was interested in wanted to get married. I didn't, so we decided to call it a day.''

''Haven't you ever wanted to settle down?''

''Of course. But only with the right woman.''

''I'm surprised she hasn't come along yet.''

''Why?'' he challenged. ''Rob didn't loom on your horizon until you were thirty.''

She looked down. ''I guess you and I are late bloomers.''

''I suppose that explanation will do for now,'' came his cryptic remark. ''It's still not too late for you to have a baby. Several babies if that's what you want. Doug's mother had four children. Her last two were born at thirty-eight and forty. You're only thirty-five.''

Why did he keep harking back to that painful subject?

''Does Doug's mother have a husband?'' she asked in a dry tone.

''Absolutely.''

''Then I rest my case. Even if I were to marry again, there's no guarantee I could get pregnant.''

''So you adopt a baby, or even an older child. Sherilyn will tell you I didn't turn out so bad as a brother.''

''She adores you.''

"And I love her."

"Graham thinks the world of you, too."

"It's mutual. I've had an upbringing worthy of any son. That's because your brother and my sister are best friends and lovers. There could be no greater combination to guarantee a happy marriage and home."

Best friends and lovers.

Those words haunted her when she thought of her own marriage. In some ways Rob had been like Mike. Married to his profession. Set in his ways. Both of them were so focused, some people mistook that trait for arrogance.

Graham wasn't like that. Even though he was an attorney, he put Sherilyn first. They shared everything and had fun together.

He'd been Zak's role model...

She moistened her dry lips nervously. "We've been talking too long. Let me help you to the bathroom. While you're in there I'll get your room cleaned up. Do you want me to put the mail in your study?"

"Yes, please."

His instant capitulation was the balm she needed right now. Their conversation had opened wounds that had only healed on the surface. She couldn't take any more emotional pounding from him tonight. He bore and bore like a woodpecker at a knothole until there was nothing left of it.

She ran the tray to the kitchen and put her passport and Jeopardy game away. All that was left to do was remake his bed and bring fresh water for his pills.

Oddly enough over the next few days Zak didn't try and question her or make innuendos about the past. It was as if the purging Tuesday night had cleared the air somehow. He talked on the phone with the family, discussed business with the men in his company, watched TV, worked on the crossword puzzles in the magazine she'd left for him.

He was constantly improving, getting his strength back. This left more time for Michelle to sunbathe on the beach and play in the ocean.

Zak had made her promise never to go out past the first curl. When he could join her, then they'd paddle out where the surfers were riding the waves.

She assured him she wouldn't be that foolish. Michelle had a healthy respect for the ocean's power. Without Zak, she wouldn't dream of going out where she could get in trouble, lifeguards or not.

For the first time in a week, he dressed in a shirt to go to the doctor's office. It was a khaki short-sleeved button down. When Michelle helped him on with it, she watched to see if he grimaced, but the effort didn't appear to cause him pain.

What a difference seven days of bed rest had made! He went out to her car and got in without any problem at all. If you didn't know his chest was wrapped underneath his shirt, you'd have no clue of the ordeal he'd been through.

The doctor's office was in a complex next to the hospital. He was a pulmonary specialist Zak said he'd only met once after the operation. As soon as they entered his empty suite, a pert redheaded receptionist, probably mid-twenties, came out to greet them.

"You must be Mr. and Mrs. Sadler."

Did Michelle really look young enough to be taken for Zak's wife?

"Come on back to the examining room. This is the

day Dr. Tebbs operates, but he told me you'd be in. He'll be here any minute.''

Michelle waited for Zak to correct the woman's erroneous assumption, but he remained silent as they followed her down the hall. Maybe he was waiting for Michelle to say something.

''I'm his nurse,'' she explained when they were shown the examining room.

''Oh— Sorry. I should know better than to speak before I leap.''

Zak smiled at the flustered receptionist. ''We don't mind at all.'' His eyes swerved to Michelle's with a mischievous gleam. ''Do we?''

''No.'' That was the only word she could articulate given the fact that Zak's question had caused her body to suffuse with heat.

''Go ahead and take off your shirt, then get up on the examining table.''

''Will you help me?'' Zak's steady gaze still clung to Michelle's.

To have refused him in front of the receptionist would have been childish, but Zak was being incorrigible today and he knew it.

No doubt it was because this was his first time out of bed, out of the house. She had no choice but to play along.

''There,'' she said once she'd undone the buttons and eased it away from his shoulders and arms.

Footsteps sounded in the hall, then the fiftyish looking doctor came in the room, still in his scrubs. He nodded to them, then eyed Zak.

''You don't look like the same man I put that tube in.''

"Michelle's given me expert nursing care at home. I feel good enough to stop taking pain killers."

"That's excellent. I'm going to unwrap this and take a look."

As Zak's chest emerged, Michelle could see the tell-tale gray and yellow signs of the bruising he'd sustained. Much to her relief, the place where the tube had been put in had healed and looked free of infection.

Dr. Tebbs took the stethoscope and listened to Zak's heart and lungs. He put him through a series of tests, including the one to find out how much air he was taking in.

When he finished his exam he said, "Ninety-seven percent. I wish all my patients recovered this quickly. All right. From now on you be the judge of how much medication you want, if any.

"You can get up and dressed every day. Feel free to move around the house, sunbathe on a patio for a little while. Eat meals at the table. No sitting for too long in one position."

"How about a stroll on the beach?"

"Not yet. No stretching, no arms over your head. No lifting, no sudden movements. Do the breathing exercises in the morning and at night.

"I want to see you back here in a week. I'll take an X-ray to look at your ribs. If everything checks out and your lungs are still filling without problem, you'll be able to go for walks."

"How soon can I get back to work?"

"Let's talk about that next Friday. Do you have any other questions?"

"I have one," Michelle spoke up. "Does he have to continue to lie on his back at night?"

The Harlequin Reader Service® — Here's how it works:

NO POSTAGE
NECESSARY
IF MAILED
IN THE
UNITED STATES

BUSINESS REPLY MAIL
FIRST-CLASS MAIL   PERMIT NO. 717-003   BUFFALO, NY

POSTAGE WILL BE PAID BY ADDRESSEE

HARLEQUIN READER SERVICE
3010 WALDEN AVE
PO BOX 1867
BUFFALO NY 14240-9952

Do You Have the LUCKY KEY?

PLAY THE Lucky Key Game
and you can get

FREE BOOKS and a FREE GIFT!

Scratch the gold areas with a coin. Then check below to see the books and gift you can get!

YES! I have scratched off the gold areas. Please send me the 2 FREE BOOKS and GIFT for which I qualify. I understand I am under no obligation to purchase any books, as explained on the back of this card.

(H-R-10/03)

386 HDL DVAH   186 HDL DVAX

FIRST NAME

LAST NAME

ADDRESS

APT.#

CITY

STATE/PROV.

ZIP/POSTAL CODE

2 free books plus a free gift

1 free book

2 free books

Try Again!

Visit us online at
www.eHarlequin.com

The doctor looked at Zak. "Are you getting restless in that position?"

"Very. But I didn't know Michelle knew it."

"A good nurse notices everything." He winked at her. "You can turn on your good side for relief as long as you don't have any trouble breathing."

"Thank goodness for that."

"Go ahead and get dressed. I'll see you in a week." He walked out.

Before the bandages had come off, Michelle wasn't as conscious of Zak's chest with its dusting of black hair. But now...it was all too much.

"As soon as we get home, let's put you in the shower and get everything washed off."

"You're reading my mind. I feel really itchy."

She finished buttoning his shirt. "I have a solution for that, too."

"I can't wait to find out what it is," his lips whispered into the silk profusion of her hair.

Their bodies and faces were so close. For one brief moment of insanity, she was tempted to lift her head and offer him her mouth.

This man was forbidden to her, yet all the reasons why she shouldn't be feeling this way about him couldn't seem to combat the aching hunger that had been building inside of her. One day soon she would have to leave, or give in to it. If that happened, then heaven help her.

"Are you two about ready to go? I have a lunch date and need to lock up."

The receptionist's voice caused Michelle to jerk away from Zak just in time. She'd almost lost it right there and begged him to kiss her. Really kiss her.

Feeling quite ill, feverish in fact, she left the examining room ahead of Zak. When she reached the door of the front office, she held it open for him while he made an appointment for the next Friday.

Next Friday it could very well be Sherilyn who brought Zak to the doctor.

Michelle had a passport. In a week she might just be thousands of miles away from California. But she had a premonition that even if she flew to Siberia, it wouldn't change certain facts.

She'd had growing feelings for Zak since seeing him again at Rob's funeral. He'd been solicitous and tender to her, urging her to talk while he listened. She'd been tempted to do just that.

Zak had a way about him. If she'd let him, he would have drawn her out, made her talk about her pain. He was that kind of man. He'd been on her mind a lot over the past twenty-four months.

Now that they'd been thrown together for the last week in such close, intimate circumstances, she recognized her feelings for what they really were.

She was in love with him, and falling harder every second they were together.

It was ludicrous.

To think that when Michelle had started second grade at Lincoln elementary school, Zak hadn't even been born yet!

CHAPTER SIX

MICHELLE hugged her brother and Sherilyn. "I'm so glad you could come for dinner again. I just wish you could stay over tonight."

"We would," Sherilyn assured her, "but Lynette's starting her new job at the sporting goods store in the morning. We need to show our support."

"Of course."

"Thank you for all you've done for Zak," her sister-in-law said. "He acts like nothing was ever wrong."

"I know. He thinks he can go surfing and jog ten miles."

"Don't you let him," Graham murmured.

"Have no fear, brother dear. I was witness to everything Dr. Tebbs told him on Friday. Please be careful driving home. Call us when you get there."

"We will." Sherilyn gave her another hug before they walked out the back door to the end of the alley where they'd parked their car.

Michelle watched until they were out of sight, then she shut and locked the door. To her surprise she heard the instrumental sounds from Bizet's Carmen wafting through the condo. Instead of finding Zak on the living room couch, she discovered he'd wandered out to the deck.

The sun had fallen into the ocean. It was one of those balmy, surreal nights, too perfect to be real.

Zak stood facing the restless surf with his legs

slightly apart, a drink in his hand. His powerful frame dressed in cutoffs was a silhouette against the twilight sky. The breathtaking image before her brought Michelle to a standstill.

Suddenly he put his glass on the table. That's when he caught her staring at him from the doorway.

"This is a magical time of night. Come and join me."

"I will as soon as I've straightened things around."

In the next instant he strolled toward her and grasped her hand. "Work can wait. This moment won't."

If she tried to pull away, she could hurt him. Side by side they went out on the deck. Because she was in shorts and a sleeveless blouse, their arms and legs brushed against each other. Fire licked through her veins.

He moved behind her, putting his hands on either side of her waist. "I hope you don't mind if I lean on you," he whispered before resting his chin on her shoulder.

Between the warmth of his breath against her cheek, and the piercingly sweet love song playing in the background, she could imagine herself dying of pleasure right there.

"How do you like it by now?"

"Do you mean Carlsbad?"

"Carlsbad...the condo..."

"You were thirteen when we first walked along this stretch of beach. I remember you telling me that one day you were going to have a home right here, and it was going to be beautiful. You've succeeded in making that dream a reality."

"Do you remember what else I said?"

She smiled in remembrance. "Yes. You asked me to

wait until you were all grown up so we could live in it together.''

''And do you remember what you said?'' he prodded.

''I promised I would.''

A tremor shook his body. ''You broke my heart when you married Rob.''

At first, the significance of his words didn't register. When they did, Michelle let out a cry. She turned around slowly.

With his body blocking the light from the living room, she couldn't see the expression in his eyes.

''You were just a boy—''

His chest heaved. ''You treated me as an equal.''

''Then the ankle bracelet—''

''Was my version of a promise ring.''

''Zak—'' Moisture filled her eyes.

''As long as you kept wearing it, I was never worried.''

A groan escaped. Without conscious thought she lifted her hands to his face. ''I hurt you when I had no idea...''

His hand caught one of hers and pressed it to his lips. ''You didn't wait for me to get all grown-up.''

A lone tear ran down her pale cheek. ''But there was nothing like that between us, Zak.''

''You were my best friend,'' his voice grated. ''That was the only relationship I understood. Your brother taught me that the best marriage partner is the one who's your best friend as well as your lover. He said you couldn't ask a woman to marry her unless you could take care of her.''

Another cry escaped her throat. ''Surely as you matured you could see I was too old for you!''

She heard his harsh intake of breath. "All I could see was that with every birthday, I was catching up to you. I believed that if I worked very hard and followed my plan to the letter, I'd attain my dream."

His confession overwhelmed her with pain. "Why are you telling me this now? I can hardly bear it."

"Why do you think?" he asked in a quieter tone. "Two years have passed since the last time we saw each other. I'm letting you know I'm finally all grown up, and can support you."

The world stood still while the words sank in.

"No, Zak," she whispered, starting to back away from him. "What you're suggesting is impossible."

"Is it? I know you loved your husband, but you and I share a very unique bond many married couples would give the world to possess. You know I'm right. We both felt that same old connection the minute you showed up at the house last week."

Her soul quaked because he was speaking the truth.

"All I ask is that you think about it while you're taking care of me."

"I don't need to think about it!" she cried in panic. "Regardless of your insistence that the family ties and the age difference don't matter to you, I have to tell you that they do matter to me.

"We've been a family for years. I've practically been a surrogate aunt to you, Zak."

His eyes narrowed. "But you're not my aunt—surrogate or otherwise—and I've never seen you as an aunt. I'm your sister-in-law's brother, not your nephew.

"As far as I'm concerned, the fact that we belong to the same family is what makes it so perfect," he reasoned in his inimitable way that had always defeated her in the past.

"We all know and love each other. We're all comfortable with each other. We enjoy each other. Today was just another case in point with Sherilyn and Graham here. For you and me to marry would be the natural progression of things."

"Natural—" she scoffed to cover her fragmented emotions. "You think it natural to marry a woman older than you, not only in terms of years, but experience?

"I assure you the whole idea goes against nature. I'm going to age long before you do. Be realistic, Zak!

"A twenty-eight-year-old man wants a young, energetic wife who can give him the best years of her life. One who has the luxury of time on her side to bear and raise children."

Silence followed her argument.

"My best years are gone!" she blurted, trying to provoke a reaction from him. "You and I would be a mismatch of Spring and Fall. The two aren't compatible. I would always be aware of time gaining on me. You would grow to hate the disparities."

"Are you quite finished?"

He spoke to her like he was the parent and she was the child who'd been having a temper tantrum.

She frowned. "You haven't heard one thing I've been saying."

"On the contrary. I know exactly how your mind works. I could have told you every word that was going to come out of your mouth before you did. As I said a few minutes ago, just give it some thought."

She was aghast. "I care about you, Zak. I don't want

to be the cause of any more hurt. By asking me to be your nurse, you've only set yourself up for more pain.''

"I've been living with it for years. I can handle it.''

"I'm afraid I can't.'' At this point she was shivering. The ocean breeze made it that much worse. She rubbed her arms for warmth. "Tomorrow I'll call home nursing services to make arrangements for a replacement.''

"If that's what you feel you have to do.''

With stunning nonchalance he walked back inside the condo, leaving her to writhe in an agony of spirit. Her eyes followed his progress until he'd disappeared from the living room.

If Zak had planted a land mine, it couldn't have done as much damage. A mine would have physically obliterated her.

This was much worse. Outwardly she was still intact. Inside she felt like a victim of shellshock.

Fifteen years ago she'd made a promise to a vulnerable thirteen-year-old boy, never dreaming of the far-reaching ramifications. He'd needed so much reassurance back then.

To a great degree Michelle had been able to relate since she and Graham had lost both their parents. It had felt natural to reach out to Zak and comfort him.

From day one they'd bonded. Their friendship grew. So did he.

Wherever she was, whatever she was doing, he would seek her out. Michelle always made time for him because she found she wanted to.

Zak was an original thinker. Fascinating. He made things fun no matter the situation. In truth, by the time he was a college freshman, she enjoyed his company more than the guys she dated. He had the quality of a good listener, one of the many traits missing in the men who wanted a relationship with her.

Then she'd met Rob, an older, attractive, eligible pediatrician who had privileges at the hospital where she worked. One of his patients, an eleven year old boy who'd broken an arm and a leg out skateboarding, had been put on the orthopedic floor.

She'd been assigned three night shifts in a row. Rob stopped by to see the boy after he'd made his pediatric rounds. He got to talking with Michelle. He showed up the next night and then the next, lingering longer with each visit.

For the first time in her adult life, Michelle met a man who had many of the qualities she'd admired in her own father before he'd been killed. As it turned out Rob, a wonderful person and caring, dedicated physician, had recently lost his grandmother. She'd been the woman who'd raised him.

After two weeks of dating, Michelle invited him home for dinner.

Rob knew how to talk to kids and was an instant hit with thirteen-year-old Lynette. Michelle could tell right away her brother respected and approved of him. She had an idea that Graham also sensed those same qualities in Rob they'd loved in their father.

Zak happened to be home that weekend which was a rarity. He behaved toward Rob the way he would with any guest. He'd shown a polite interest in him.

The next day when Zak asked her to go to a swimming party with him at his friend Carl's apartment, she told him she couldn't go because Rob was picking her up at any moment.

Now that she recalled the moment, it seemed like

there was a long pregnant silence before Zak grabbed his beach towel and left the house without saying another word to her. But at that time she'd been too involved with Rob to worry about it.

Within six weeks she and Rob were engaged, and a frenzy of activity followed to plan a church wedding with a traditional white wedding dress and all the trimmings.

Michelle asked Lynette and two other friends to be bridesmaids. Gail, her best friend since grade school, served as her maid of honor. Rob's cousin, Randy, stood in as best man. Graham gave Michelle away.

Zak, whom she'd seen nothing of since the night she'd brought Rob home for dinner, sat with his sister during the ceremony. Afterward he helped her with the reception which was held on the patio behind the church.

When it came time for Michelle to leave on her honeymoon with Rob, Zak approached her and kissed her cheek. "I hope you're happy," was all he'd said before disappearing.

That was five long years ago...

Michelle looked out at the ocean waves forming in tiers, haunted by the knowledge that Zak had loved her all that time before her marriage, yet he'd kept silent.

The words he'd said to her at the reception held a completely different meaning for her now. When he'd whispered them, he'd been in agony. Her heart felt the wrench.

They had to talk!

She grabbed the glass off the table and closed the sliding door. Zak had left the music on. She shut it off before cleaning up the kitchen.

With everything done, she headed for his bedroom to check him over before she put him through his exercises.

When she walked in, she discovered he'd already showered. He was just getting into bed wearing the bottom half of his pajamas. In two days his bruises had faded even more. The spot where the tube had been put in was tiny. In time the scar would fade.

They'd been through the routine so many times before, he automatically rolled the pillow up against his chest and began coughing for her. No one watching them would have any idea how he'd rocked her world tonight with his admissions.

After she'd taken his blood pressure and listened to his lungs, she sat down on the side of the bed. His benign expression gave away none of his feelings.

"Zak?" She took his right hand between hers. For the moment all she could see was the young teenager she'd befriended years ago. Tenderness darkened the blue of her eyes.

"I've had enough time to absorb everything you told me out on the deck. You took me by surprise, and I said the first thing that came into my head. Be assured I'm not going to leave you until the doctor says you can resume a normal life.

"You're not in love with me," she began. "Like Lynette whose feelings for you are all mixed up between hero worship and reality, I'm afraid I became something more in your eyes at a time in your life when you needed security so badly.

"Now it appears the shoe's on the other foot. Rob is gone. You feel sorry for me because I'm alone. You want to comfort *me*.

"There's no question that over the years we've both learned to love each other, Zak. You've always meant the world to me. When you asked me to be your nurse, I was glad that I was free to help you. Not only because I wanted to assist you with the care you needed, but because I've missed you."

She kissed the tips of his fingers before letting his hand go. "I think it's providential you told me what you did tonight. What you said touched me more than words can say.

"I believe it was cathartic for you too. Now we can put the past behind us and move on as friends who've been through a lot, both together and apart."

His chest expanded with the breath he took. "You'll always be my best friend, Michelle."

"And you mine," she admitted.

These intimate confessions should have happened between her and Rob, but once he'd found out he was dying, he'd closed up and kept her at arm's length, unwittingly crushing her love.

When Zak had talked to her at the funeral, she'd sensed he would never have been like Rob. He would have shared everything with her until his last breath, the way they'd shared everything until she'd gotten involved with her nursing career and their lives had gone down different paths.

"You were right about the bond we share. When I saw you at the house, it was like old times years ago."

Zak nodded. Suddenly he looked happier. "I have an idea. Remember when you were on vacation for two weeks and we had a Boggle tournament that lasted the whole time?"

She groaned. "How could I forget? I could never

make as many words out of those darn cubes as you no matter how hard I tried.''

"Let's have one this week starting in the morning after breakfast.''

"You're on! That is, *if* you can promise me you haven't been playing a version of it on your office computer.''

His deep laughter resonated to her bones. "I swear it.''

"Good, because I've had years of practice at that game since the last time you defeated me.''

His smile widened into a wicked grin. "The loser has to take the other one out to dinner next Friday night at the winner's choice of location. By then I'll have my doctor's permission.''

"I have no doubt of it as long as you continue to recover without complications." She got up from the bed. "I'll bring you some ice water. Is there anything else I can get for you?''

"Not a thing, thank you.''

On the way back to his room she heard his cell phone ring. It was his sister calling to let him know they'd arrived home safely. Michelle put his drink on the bedside table and whispered goodnight.

Next door in her own bedroom, she drew the curtain and opened the sliding door. After getting ready for bed, she turned out the lights and lay down to watch the ocean.

She should have been exhausted after the emotional evening Zak had put her through, yet sleep was the last thing on her mind. Going to his bedroom to talk things out had been the right thing to do about an impossible situation.

By drawing a parallel between him and Lynette, hopefully Michelle had made him realize he'd been living the tail end of a fantasy that had gone on too long. He was a grown man now and could think with a grown man's rationale.

Even if Graham and Sherilyn found nothing wrong with their brother and sister getting together, they'd be the first to say Zak's destiny lay with a much younger woman.

The teenage Zak had only seen what he'd wanted to see. The man in the next room was a big boy now. He didn't really want some worn out nurse for his lifetime companion.

When Friday rolled around and Zak had declared himself the winner of the Boggle tournament, Michelle was quick to point out that her mind was keeping pace with the aging process. In his triumphant mood, he let the comment ride.

Dr. Tebbs made Zak's day even more exciting when he said the X-ray looked good. So did his lungs. At this point his patient should be taking daily walks to build up his strength. After each session Michelle should test his oxygen intake and continue to monitor his vital signs.

No driving the car yet, no swimming in the ocean, no going back to work. Zak was to come in for another appointment the following week.

"Where am I supposed to drive us for this surprise dinner treat?" It was six in the evening when she backed her car out of the garage. Zak had dressed himself in a brushed cotton zip mock turtleneck and pleated lightweight wool trousers. Both were in a tan color.

With Zak's arresting looks and physique, it didn't matter whether he was wearing an outfit like this or simple cutoffs. The other men around simply didn't measure up.

"Head for Oceanside. We'll park near the old pier and walk to the restaurant at the end of it."

"I remember that place. It feels like you're on a ship out on the ocean. As I recall, they had good fish and chips."

"That's what I'm craving."

When they reached the area in question, it didn't look too crowded yet. Michelle was able to park the car near the crosswalk that led to the famous old pier. She sensed Zak's eagerness to stretch his legs after such a long siege of inactivity. With the temperature in the low seventies, a leisurely walk sounded good to her, too.

Halfway to the end she noticed fishermen on both sides of the pier. She paused at the railing for a minute to see if they were catching anything. Probably not with all the surfers out riding the last few waves before dark.

"Black's your best color," Zak murmured. She turned in his direction and discovered him watching her through eyes that had taken on the green of the ocean. "It must be a new outfit. You look terrific."

Her breathing grew shallow. "Thank you. You look pretty gorgeous yourself."

The salesgirl had talked Michelle into the black corduroy boot cut pants. She'd brought out a black and white striped open neck shirt to go with it. The French cuffs made it a little dressier.

When Michelle had questioned that the outfit probably suited a younger woman, the salesgirl laughed at her before showing her to a mirror. In the end Michelle had broken down and bought a pair of black wedges to go with the pants.

"In the setting sun your hair is the most amazing mixture of silver and gold."

She started to say something, but he put a finger to her lips.

"For once don't spoil the moment by making a disparaging remark about your age. I don't see any gray hairs yet."

He'd read her mind with uncanny perception.

By tacit agreement they began walking again. When it grew crowded, he took her arm to guide her. She felt the stares of people watching their progress.

Michelle was oblivious to the men's attention. All she could see were the women who eyed Zak with unabashed female interest.

It occurred to her she was no longer the nurse helping him to get around so he wouldn't fall. They looked like a couple out to enjoy the evening together.

Enjoy it she did.

They both ate fish and chips topped off with double malted chocolate shakes. From their window they could see sailboats in the distance. The ocean swells caused the pier to sway the tiniest bit, giving the impression they were on the high seas.

"How do you feel?" she asked when they'd finished eating. "If you're tired from the walk, we can catch one of the carts and be driven back to the car."

"To be truthful, I can't remember the last time I felt more alive and rested."

"Sherilyn told me you haven't taken a vacation in several years."

"She told me the same thing about you."

Michelle looked down at her empty plate. "I wouldn't have wished this accident on you, but since it did happen, this long break has been good for you."

"Ditto." He left cash for the waitress. "Shall we go? Our evening has only begun."

Her heart began to palpitate. "What do you mean?"

A mysterious smile broke the corners of his mouth. "You'll find out."

When they reached the crosswalk, Michelle would have headed for the car, but Zak grasped her arm.

"There's a special performance going on in the little open-air amphitheater two blocks from here. Let's walk up there. I know you'll enjoy it."

"If you're sure you're not feeling tired."

"I'll let you know if that happens."

"Promise?"

His eyes pierced hers. "Have I ever lied to you?"

"No."

"Then let's go."

He grasped her hand as they crossed the street. When they reached the other side she expected him to release her, but he didn't. With so many college kids and young people invading the beach for the weekend, she supposed this was his way of protecting her.

Closer to their destination she picked out the sounds of island music. She glanced at Zak.

"That's Miki's family and all his cousins and their families. Periodically they put on a fabulous show here for the city. You have to buy the tickets ahead of time. It's already started, but Melee promised to save us seats down in front. Come on. Let's hurry."

Excited, Michelle picked up her pace to stay astride of Zak. When they reached the stage area and had found their places, she counted thirty people including Miki's children in full Tongan ceremonial dress.

It was growing dark. The tiki torches illuminated their beautiful faces and bodies. Between the exciting war dances with the drums, and the many enchanting love songs, Michelle was transported to Tonga for a little while.

When they did their concluding number, the ovation was thundrous. After the din subsided, Miki announced they would pipe their recorded music through the PA system so everyone could dance who wanted to.

Their performance had attracted a huge crowd. People spilled out into the street to sway to the music.

"Hey, Zak—"

Michelle whirled around in time to see Miki and Melee making their way over to them. Their children followed.

He shook Zak's hand. "We're glad you came."

"We wouldn't have missed it," Zak assured him.

"It was so wonderful!" Michelle cried. When she spotted the two boys, she hugged them. "Your voices are gorgeous. Unbelievably beautiful."

Melee beamed. "You're looking good, Zak. Here. This is for you." She put a flowered lei around his neck. Her husband did the same to Michelle who buried her nose in the flowers to inhale the fragrance.

"Thank you," they both said at the same time.

"Does this mean you'll be back at work on Monday?"

"I'm afraid not. Give me one more week."

"Hey—being home agrees with you. Take two more weeks," Melee urged. She had a gleam in her dark eyes as she eyed both of them.

Michelle bent down. "How would you boys like to dance?"

Amato giggled, but Selu, the younger one, nodded.

"Come on then." She led him around a small area of the dance floor, much to the delight of the crowd. Pretty soon Amato ran over and wanted his turn.

When she finally returned him to his smiling parents, she was flushed. "They're adorable."

Melee put her hands on her hips. "You're good with kids."

"Shall we find out how good she is with me?" Zak teased before spiriting her on to the floor.

Michelle had done many activities with Zak over the years, but they'd never danced before.

The evening was already enchanted. She knew she shouldn't be doing this, but somehow she found herself gravitating to him without conscious thought. Just one dance, she told herself.

"Don't lift your arms, Zak!"

His shuttered eyes played over her upturned features. "We'll just hold each other."

He slid his arms around her waist, pulling her close. It forced her to slide hers around his neck. Her cheek pressed against the flowers of his lei, releasing their intoxicating scent.

Their bodies molded together. He felt too good. He was like a drug she couldn't get enough of. Slowly they moved around the dance floor to the sounds of one heavenly Tongan love song after another.

"This is nice, isn't it?" He'd buried his face in her hair.

"Yes." If she said any more, she was afraid her voice would shake from the desire he'd aroused by just being

Zak. "I think we'd better stop soon. You've done more than you should today."

"You're the nurse. Let me know when you want to leave."

I never want to leave.

I never want to stop holding you like this.

I never want you to stop holding me like this.

"Y-your breathing sounds shallow," she stammered.

"So does yours. Maybe if I do this, it will solve the problem."

She let out a helpless little cry as Zak's mouth moved across her feverish cheek to cover her own.

It wasn't like the gentle brush of his lips against hers a week ago. Their mouths fused with the searing heat of long-suppressed passion. She clung to him with mindless abandon, unaware that they'd stopped dancing.

The spiral which had been bringing her closer and closer to him had sucked her into a vortex of sensual ecstasy.

"That's been coming for a long time," he said on a ragged breath, finally lifting his mouth from hers. His eyes looked glazed over. "Thank you for not fighting me. You've been my fantasy for too many years.

"Now that I've gotten that out of my system, I think I can go back to being your friend. Shall we say good night to the Mokofisis?"

CHAPTER SEVEN

IT WAS close to eleven when Michelle and Zak reached her car for the short drive back to Carlsbad.

Since leaving the amphitheater, he hadn't tried to hold her hand or engage her in small talk. In fact he'd walked along with a detached air of contentment while she—

There was only one way to describe her condition.

She was dying inside.

The terrible thing that should never have happened, *had* happened. Zak had scaled the last defense which in the past had helped her hold her ground. Now he knew her weakness.

He knew all about it, her inner voice cried.

They'd barely pulled away from the curb when his cell phone went off. He drew it from his trouser pocket. The moment he spoke she could tell it was Sherilyn.

"Hold on a second. Let me check with Michelle." He turned to her.

"It's Lynette's birthday tomorrow."

"That's right!" She'd thought about it the other day, but then it had slipped from her mind.

"They think it might be good if you and I drove to Riverside in the morning to celebrate. We could stay through Sunday so the car ride is split up over two days."

After what had gone on tonight, the invitation couldn't have come at a more propitious moment.

"It's an inspired idea," Michelle said. "Even if Lynette leaves the house or refuses to participate, she'll know you came because you wanted to help celebrate her birthday."

He put the phone to his ear once more. "Michelle's in full agreement. We'll be there about eleven." They spoke for another minute, then he hung up.

"I'm afraid I don't have a gift for her yet," she lamented.

"That makes two of us." Zak rested his head against the back of the seat. Michelle hoped he was only pleasantly tired. "When we reach Riverside, we can stop at a store and buy her a couple of the latest CDs for her car."

"Maybe we could pick up a movie, too. Under the circumstances we need to get you to bed the minute we arrive at the condo."

"I can hear the alarm in your voice, Michelle. Relax. I can't remember the last time I felt this good."

Neither can I. That's why I can't ever let another night like this happen again.

When they drove in the alley, Zak asked her to stop so he could get out and bring in the mail. He'd meet her inside the condo.

The relief of being alone to put the car away gave her the few minutes she needed to get hold of herself. Certain words had been going around in her head like a litany.

Now that I've gotten that out of my system, I think I can go back to being your friend.

If Zak could do that, then he wasn't made of flesh and blood.

But she knew he *was*.

That kiss had changed everything for her.

She was frightened. She needed someone to talk to this weekend. Someone who'd seen a lot of life already. A good friend she could trust. Someone who could be objective, who wouldn't judge her.

Deep in thought, she entered Zak's bedroom a few minutes later. She found him in front of the screen, staring out at the ocean.

She reached for the blood pressure cup. "Come on. We'll make this quick."

When he turned, she noticed immediately there was something different about him since he'd come in the house.

He had a cold, brooding look on his face. She hadn't seen that look in years...not since he'd been a young teen trying to make sense of his life.

Her heart dropped to her feet. "What's wrong, Zak?"

Silence greeted her question. She put the blood pressure cup down again. "Has there been bad news? Did you get another phone call from Sherilyn while you were out at the mailbox?"

"No," he muttered, before facing the ocean once more.

"Then something must have come in the mail that disturbed you," she prodded.

"I appreciate your concern, but I don't want to talk about it."

She bit her lip. Though she knew this drastic change in him wasn't because of anything she'd done, she still felt rejected in a very painful, personal way. In retrospect, she realized he'd never excluded her from anything before.

Tonight had been filled with firsts that had left her reeling.

"I need to take your vital signs."

"Not now," came the withering response.

She'd been dismissed.

On her way out of the room she saw that he'd put the lei on the dresser next to the gardenia plant. While she breathed in the combined scents of the flowers, she spied the corner of an envelope beneath the petals that hadn't been there earlier.

Suddenly her feet refused to move. Something traumatic was going on inside of him. She was determined to find out what it was.

"Zak—"

He wheeled around wooden faced. "Why are you still in here?"

She'd never seen him like this before. "Because you're in pain. Last week you accused me of closing up. Now you're doing the same thing. Talk to me, Zak," she begged.

A grimace carved lines in his face making him appear older. It took him a long time before he spoke.

"I received a letter from a law firm in Los Angeles."

Fear clutched at her heart. "Is your company being sued?"

"No."

"Thank heaven for that." Her voice throbbed.

She couldn't stop her mind from grasping at any remote possibility that would explain his forbidding countenance.

Maybe a woman from his past had filed a paternity suit against him. The abhorrent idea suffused her with agony.

When she thought she couldn't stand the suspense any longer he said, "It would appear my birthfather is alive and has been searching for me."

His birthfather...

She gasped softly.

"But this is incredible. How on earth did he know where to find you?"

"Perhaps the salient question is, *how long* has he known where to find me?" came the voice of ice.

A shudder attacked her body. "What else did the letter say?"

"He would like to meet his son, however his name has been withheld for reasons of confidentiality. All I have to do is let the attorney know my wishes. If I'm not interested, then I'll never be bothered again."

Michelle hugged her arms to her waist in consternation.

She could only imagine the turmoil this information had created. He'd suffered so much emotional damage at the death of his adoptive parents, not to mention that his birthparents had given him up to foster care, it was a miracle he'd been able to overcome it.

But the scars had always been there, buried deep in his psyche. It wasn't fair that with one letter, they'd been ripped apart.

Sucking in her breath she said, "You wouldn't be human if you weren't curious about him, especially when you were never told the circumstances that put you in the hands of social services."

He flashed her a dark, sardonic glance. "It's a moot point now. What he and my birthmother did to me was inhuman."

Oh, Zak—

Michelle's heart went out to him. "Perhaps it's been weighing him down all these years."

One dark brow lifted scornfully. "Death bed repentance you mean."

"Maybe. If he's dying…"

"Do you think I give a damn?" his voice shook.

"Yes," she answered honestly. "Because of him you have life."

He turned toward the ocean once more. Michelle moved closer to him.

"If you're worried about Sherilyn's reaction, you don't have to be. Whatever your decision, she'll be behind it a thousand percent. She's always had your best interest at heart. So has Graham."

"You think I don't know that?" he demanded with a violence driven by pain.

"I'm saying all the wrongs things. I'm not in your shoes and don't know what it feels like. Forgive me, Zak," she whispered before darting from the room.

Bed was no sanctuary, but there was nowhere else to go with all the emotions tearing her apart.

The kiss she and Zak had shared tonight was like opening Pandora's box, unleashing a force that terrified her. Now a missive had arrived for him from out of the blue.

If he chose to meet his father, who knew what other forces lay in wait to bring more upheaval. Depending on what he found out, it could change him.

It *would* change him. Of course it would. But how? That was the question she wrestled with for the rest of the night.

Sleep never came because she knew she wasn't the only one struggling. On the other side of the wall, a man was fighting his old demons and there wasn't a thing she could do to help him. But when he greeted her the next morning, he acted as if nothing had happened.

That wasn't like Zak. But this situation was different than anything he'd ever faced. She had to accept the fact that it would be on his time table if he chose to tell her anything at all.

After a quick breakfast, they left the condo at nine. En route they made desultory conversation and listened to the radio. In Riverside they stopped to buy Lynette's presents and have them gift-wrapped.

Once that was accomplished they drove to the house where Graham and Sherilyn were out in front pulling some weeds. The four of them congregated in the driveway.

Everyone was thrilled at the progress Zak was making. Eventually the conversation got around to Lynette.

"She had to be at the store early this morning, but she only has to work part-time today." Sherilyn glanced at her watch. "She should be back home by one-thirty."

"Then let's get busy on the party for her." Michelle put an arm through hers and they entered the house. The men followed.

"What are you giving her for a present?"

To Michelle's surprise Sherilyn looked a little sheepish before she sought her husband's gaze. "You tell her, darling."

Graham eyed Michelle frankly. "Sherilyn's nervous to tell you because she doesn't want you to be hurt in any way."

"About what?" Zak asked before Michelle could form the words.

"After you married Rob, Lynette wanted to move into your apartment. We told her she was too young and made it clear it was still yours whether you lived here or not. End of subject.

"Since then many things have changed, not the least of which is our daughter. After a great deal of thought, we moved all her things in the apartment as soon as she left for work this morning."

"I'm so glad!" Michelle cried out.

"You're sure you don't mind?"

"Sherilyn— How can you even ask me that? When I come for visits, I'll stay in her old bedroom. The important thing here is that this shows you trust her. She can be independently dependent, the same way I was."

Everyone chuckled.

Zak put an arm around his sister. "I agree with Michelle. It's the best present you could have given her."

"She may still go apartment hunting," Sherilyn bemoaned.

Graham smiled. "Even if she does, she'll have to live in our apartment until she's earned enough money for a first and last month's rent on a different place. Many's the slip between cup and lip."

Michelle smiled back. "Dad used to say that. Let's hope in this case you're right." She turned to Sherilyn. "Now let me help with dinner."

"I've already made the salads. We'll barbecue chicken and eat out on the patio."

"What can I do?"

"Frost the cake."

"My favorite job," Michelle quipped, leaving the

men behind while she joined her sister-in-law in the kitchen.

When quarter to two rolled around and Lynette still hadn't arrived, Sherilyn called the store to see if she'd been delayed. By the pained look on her face when she hung up the receiver, everyone knew Lynette was somewhere else.

Zak pursed his lips. "Did you tell her I was coming home?"

"Not in so many words. She knew we were planning a birthday dinner."

"Well I'm starving!" Graham declared. "We'll proceed as if she were here, and hope she shows up at some point."

A half hour later Lynette walked out on the patio where everyone was enjoying second and third helpings of food. The gifts were piled at her place waiting to be opened.

Graham started to sing happy birthday. The rest of them joined in.

After the last note she glanced at her parents. "What's happened to my room?"

"Funny you should ask," her father said. He dangled a key in front of her. "This is for you."

Lynette's pretty face didn't look so pretty when she frowned. "I don't understand."

"Every nineteen year old should have her own apartment."

Her expression tautened. "I don't want Aunt Michelle's."

"It's not hers anymore. You can paint it, redecorate it, do whatever you want to make it yours."

"I'd take it while the going's good," Zak inserted

smoothly. "Do you have any idea how lucky you are to have a father who has loved you from the moment he knew Sherilyn was carrying you?

"Who was there to see you born? Who walked you to kindergarten on your first day? Who told you that you would always be his princess no matter how many mean things your friends said to hurt you?"

Stillness permeated the atmosphere.

Michelle lowered her head. No one but she knew what had prompted Zak's emotional remarks. But until, or if, he enlightened the family, her lips were sealed.

"You ought to be down on your knees thanking God for your parents." He reached in his pocket. "Do you know what this is?"

When Michelle looked up, she saw he was holding the letter that had been lying under the lei last night.

"It came to my office and was forwarded to the condo yesterday afternoon. Take it, Lynette. Open it, and read it to everyone."

A white-faced Lynette was so intimidated, she did her uncle's bidding. After unfolding the letter she began reading.

"Dear Mr. Sadler, my name is Rex Jamison, attorney-at-law with the firm of Walters, McKnight and Jamison, in Los Angeles, California.

"My client, who shall remain nameless at this juncture, has asked me to write to you on his behalf. After making inquiries, he has the proof that you are his... son."

While Lynette stood there in shock, Sherilyn's gasp turned everyone's heads. Graham's expression didn't change, but Michelle saw something flicker in the depths of his eyes.

"Keep reading," Zak told Lynette.

"H-he would like to meet with you," she stammered, "but he understands if you don't want anything—" Lynette paused because tears had started to roll down her pale cheeks "—understands if you don't want anything to do with him," she finally finished the sentence.

"P-please inform this office of your wishes. If you choose not to meet with him, my client assures you he won't try to make further contact or bother you in any way.

"Sincerely, Rex Jamison."

Zak took the letter back from her. "That is *my* father, Lynette. I'd say he's about twenty-eight years too late. Wouldn't you?

"But *your* dad was there to see my third place win at the science fair, and watch me throw the javelin at the high school track meet.

"He was the one who helped me move into my college dorm, and slipped money in my sock drawer when I wasn't looking. His was the face I saw next to Sherilyn's when I regained consciousness after the accident, telling me I was going to be fine."

His hazel eyes were suspiciously bright. "Don't abandon your parents the way my birthparents abandoned me, Lynette. Life's too precious."

At this point Graham and Sherilyn were completely dissolved. Lynette, who'd broken down sobbing, turned to both of them to beg their forgiveness.

Michelle's wet gaze gravitated to Zak's. She couldn't take him in her arms, so she did the next best thing and reached for his hand. He grasped it in a grip so tight she was sure he didn't realize how much pressure he was exerting.

"Are you going to meet him?" Lynette asked in a quiet voice a few minutes later.

By now she'd seated herself at her place. Zak had accomplished a miracle. Lynette was speaking to him again, and she'd made peace with her parents.

"That decision is up to Michelle."

Michelle heard herself mentioned and almost fainted.

"She was the first friend I made when Graham bought this house for all of us to live in. In truth, she forced me to be her friend. I was a touchy, super sensitive nine year old whose difficult behavior left a lot to be desired.

"I gave her the hardest time I could, but deep down I kept praying she wouldn't give up on me."

Zak, Zak.

"From an early age she became my closest friend, and more recently my nurse. She's always known what was good for me.

"To answer your question, birthday girl, if she thinks it's better to let sleeping dogs lie, then I trust her judgment implicitly. You see, my true family is sitting right here. I don't need or want anyone else."

There were hidden messages in the speech he'd just given Lynette. Messages meant for Michelle to ponder.

All I ask is that you think about it.

The whole time Lynette opened presents, Michelle was very much aware that Zak hadn't given up on the fantasy that eventually they'd get married. Quite the contrary.

She had to get out of the house, away from his overpowering influence.

"Everybody?" Michelle announced. "While you

guys take everything to Lynette's apartment, I'll clean up here, then I'm going to visit my friend Gail.''

Michelle had said the first name that came into her head.

''I probably won't be back until late, but since I have a key, I'll let myself in and go to bed upstairs.''

''What about my vital signs?''

Zak hadn't been worried about them last night.

Without looking at him she said, ''I'll check them in the morning after you've taken a walk.''

She jumped up from the table and started carrying the dishes into the kitchen. To her relief Zak had little choice but to help the others.

Thankful there wasn't a great deal to be done, she was able to escape from the house before Zak could come looking for her.

It wasn't until she'd backed out of the driveway and was halfway down the street that she let go of the breath she was holding. They'd been together so constantly, she was on the verge of losing her mind.

When she reached the coast highway, she pulled her Audi into a full service gas station and stopped in front of a set of pumps. After the attendant filled her tank, she used her cell phone to call the one person who might be able to give her help. What she needed was a man's perspective on a situation growing out of control.

She phoned Mike at home but got his voice message. Most likely he was at the golf course. On the hope she might catch him there, she obtained the number through information and called the golf shop.

When she announced that she was Mike Francis's former nurse and needed to get in touch with him, the manager told her Mike was out on the links and would probably be there for another couple of hours.

She thanked him and hung up. If she left for Murrieta right now, she could be there in forty-five minutes.

How right Zak had been when he'd told Lynette what a lucky girl she was to have Graham. A girl needed her father at a time like this. If Michelle's dad were still alive, she would turn to him. Mike was going to have to play substitute.

Poor Mike. He'd told her she could come to him if she ever needed help. Little did he know she was about to take him up on his unselfish proposition. Because there'd always been honesty between them, she had the assurance the offer had been genuine.

The sun hung a little lower in the sky when she drove in the parking lot of the golf shop. No sooner had she climbed out of the driver's seat than Mike waved to her from the doorway. The manager must have told him she'd phoned.

They both started toward each other. He looked tanned and fit. With his limp barely noticeable, it wouldn't be long before he was almost as good as new.

''Mike—''

They hugged.

''I know you wouldn't be here unless you needed to talk. Follow me home where we can be private. The press have been really intrusive this afternoon.''

That was all Michelle needed to hear before hurrying back to the car.

Five minutes later she sat across from him in the living room, a place where they'd spent weeks together during his therapy.

''Would you like a cola?''

"Nothing for me thank you."

Mike studied her for a minute. "You look wonderful, but your eyes have a haunted quality I've never seen before. Tell me about this man you're in love with."

She buried her face in her hands. "It's my sister-in-law's adopted brother, Zak."

"Ah. So he's the untouchable one."

"Yes," she confessed. "He's only twenty-eight years old. He claims he's been in love with me for years and has this preposterous idea that he wants to marry me."

"What's so preposterous about it?" Mike asked in such a reasonable tone she wanted to scream. He sounded just like Zak!

Her head reared back. "Everything! We've been a family. I'm sure my brother and his wife would be shocked."

"But he's not a blood relative. You're as free to marry him as your brother was to marry his wife. I don't see the problem and I doubt they would either. If you marry Zak, you'll go on being a family."

Zak had said virtually the same thing.

"What else has you so upset?"

She took a struggling breath. "Think of a woman you know who's seven or eight years older than you are."

"Dena Margetts," he said right off.

Michelle blinked. "That good looking female pro golfer?"

He nodded with a smile.

"Well maybe she's attractive right now, but she's going to get old. If you were to marry her today, it might not be so bad. However several years down the road and—"

"*I* would be several years down the road too," he finished the sentence for her.

"Be honest," her voice shook. "If you could marry anyone, you would never choose an older woman!"

"If I were in love with her, of course I would. What difference does it make when you're both adults? Statistics prove that most women outlive their husbands by seven or eight years. Were you to marry Zak, you'd probably enjoy his companionship until the very end of your life which would be the best of all possible worlds."

"You don't understand. My skin isn't as smooth anymore. I have lines and wrinkles that a twenty-two-year-old woman doesn't have. It's harder for me to lose weight. I puff more when I walk. I have some gray hairs.

"Come on, I don't possess that dewy look of a twenty-two-year-old who's at the most beautiful she will ever be in her life."

His expression sobered. "How old was Zak when your brother married?"

"Nine."

"Then he's seen you through every stage of smooth skin, toned body including that dewy look. He didn't miss out. He loved you then, he loves you now."

Her eyes smarted. "He wants children. I'll be thirty-six next birthday. I'm not even sure if I'm fertile."

"Then marry him quick and find out. Have you considered it might have been your husband who couldn't give you a baby? His disease could have affected him. While you're hoping to get pregnant, put in the papers to adopt."

"Zak shouldn't have to adopt a child, not when he

was adopted himself. A younger woman could give him all the children he wants.''

Mike sat forward in the chair eyeing her with compassion. ''You know something? You're skirting the real issue here.''

Her heart skipped a beat. ''What do you mean?''

''Admit that deep down you're afraid you won't please him in all the ways a wife wants to please her husband, if you know what I mean. Zak's younger than Rob. You're nervous about meeting his expectations. Am I right?''

She averted her eyes.

Mike had just zeroed in on the one thing that tortured her whenever she allowed herself to think about it.

''That's an area where no one can help you. But if it's any consolation, just imagine how he feels. Men get frightened, too, you know.''

''Frightened—Zak?''

''He's aware you loved your husband and had a satisfying relationship with him. I can guarantee he's worried about how he'll compare, not only as a lover, but as a companion.

''Your husband was a fine doctor, Michelle. Mature, nice looking. You're a terrific nurse. Your professions were compatible.

''I can promise you Zak has been asking himself if he can make you as happy as you were with Rob. Will he be able to keep you happy over a lifetime?''

Michelle had never thought of Zak as having any fears. He was such a self-confident man. She'd been so focused on her own inadequacies, it had never occurred to her he would have the kinds of reservations Mike was talking about.

That's why she'd instinctively come to Mike rather than Gail for answers.

"Love hit hard after you agreed to be his nurse."

She swallowed hard. "Yes. Before taking care of him, the last time I saw him was at Rob's funeral two years ago. I'd hit rock bottom because Rob hadn't let me in to help him emotionally.

"I'm afraid I made comparisons between him and Zak who has always been so easy to talk to, and I felt guilty about it. Zak's been on my mind ever since."

"Then marry the poor guy!"

"He asked me to think about our future. Now I can't think about anything else," she admitted.

"I'd like to meet Zak one day. He must have a warrior's heart to keep coming after you despite everything you've said and done to discourage him the last few weeks. Sounds like the worthiest of competitors. I'm just grateful he's not a pro golfer."

"Oh Mike—" She stood up, half laughing, half crying. "You're so wonderful. I needed this talk more than you'll ever know."

"I needed you more than you'll ever know when I came home from the hospital. Those were dark, depressing days. You gave me the hope I could play golf again. For that I'll always be grateful, Michelle, so I guess we're even.

"Come on. I'll walk you out to your car."

CHAPTER EIGHT

"I THOUGHT you said you went to visit Gail yesterday."

How did Zak know she hadn't?

With her pulse racing too fast, Michelle looked up from the sandwiches she'd just made for their lunch. A grim-faced Zak stood next to the kitchen counter with a section of the Sunday newspaper in hand.

Much to her consternation and the family's disappointment, he'd awakened early that morning, anxious to return to Carlsbad. They all recognized that the letter from the attorney had put him in his restless state. There was nothing for Michelle to do but pack up and leave with him after breakfast.

The trip home had been pleasant enough. They'd avoided the subject eating at him. Instead they'd talked about the positive change in Lynette's behavior. Graham and Sherilyn seemed to be new people. Things were good. Or so she'd thought...

"That was my original intention, but then I changed my mind."

"I guess you did," his voice grated.

He thrust the sports page at her. The second she looked down, she groaned out loud. There in black and white was a picture of her and Mike hugging outside the golf shop.

The headline read, *Could a new romance be in the wind for Pro Golf star Mike Francis?*

Beneath the picture it said, *According to the manager*

of the golf shop in Murrieta, the beautiful blonde is none other than his nurse Michelle Howard who gave him specialized therapy after he broke his leg. Is it any wonder he sprang back from his unfortunate accident in such great shape?

Rumor has it she'll be in Sydney rooting for Mike at his first tournament since his recovery. What better incentive to take home the winner's cup for this champion who's rated third in the world.

"The press got it wrong as usual." She put the newspaper aside and went over to the sink to wash her hands.

"But they didn't get the picture wrong, did they," he muttered.

"No."

Zak couldn't possibly know how desperate she'd been to talk to Mike yesterday. He'd understood that desperation. It was a friend's arms that had gone around her.

"Do you want to eat in the dining room or out on the patio?"

"Has the time spent with me made you realize you really are in love with him?" Zak had completely ignored her question.

Her breath froze in her lungs. If Mike hadn't pointed out that Zak was as vulnerable as she was, she wouldn't have picked up on the fear underlining his question.

"I told you before I'm not in love with him. That hasn't changed. I had another reason for going to see him, but the timing was bad because it's evident a journalist was still on the premises and caught us greeting each other."

Shadows darkened his face. "Do you always throw your arms around your former patients?" he demanded.

"Yes," came the honest reply. "When you special nurse someone who's lived through a traumatic experience, you develop a bond."

He raked a hand through his black hair distractedly.

"If you wanted to talk to someone, why didn't you come to me?"

Mike had been right about everything. Zak was hurt because in his eyes, she had needs he couldn't fill.

But how could Michelle give him the answer he wanted to hear until she'd felt out her brother and sister-in-law on a certain delicate subject first?

"You have enough on your mind right now, Zak."

"If you're talking about my birthfather, that's not the reason you didn't choose to confide in me, or ask my help or whatever in the hell you thought Mike could do for you."

"I don't know why I didn't figure it out before now," he muttered bleakly. "I'm not Rob or even a little bit like him."

Her eyes closed tightly.

"Before you came down to breakfast this morning, I told the family you've helped me to the point where I don't need a nurse anymore. They're expecting you back at your house later in the day."

Michelle had just been given her walking orders.

The only way she could bear it was the fact that if there was the slightest hope for a marriage between them, then this separation would be temporary. But Zak didn't know that, her heart cried.

"How will you handle getting groceries?"

"Doug and Miki will be coming in and out of the condo this next week."

"You've got a doctor's appointment on Friday."

"I'll drive myself." His eyes darted to the sandwiches. "If you'll wrap those up and put them in the fridge, I'll eat them when I get back from my walk."

He was on the verge of bolting. Over the years of knowing Zak, she recognized the signs. "How long are you going to be gone?"

"That depends. I have a friend who lives about a half mile down the beach from here. I found out she's home from vacation so I'll probably stay and talk to her for a while."

"About your birthfather?" Michelle knew he needed to sort through his feelings with someone.

He shot her a penetrating glance. "No. I was waiting for your input during the drive home in the car."

"That's not my right, Zak." She got the foil out of the drawer to put the sandwiches away. "No matter what you said in front of the family, no one could possibly know what you should do except you. But if you want to talk about it while I'm packing, I'd be happy to listen."

His smile didn't reach his eyes. "You're the perfect nurse. Dutiful to the end." He breathed deeply. "There are no words that can adequately express my gratitude. Hopefully the check you receive in a few days will show the extent of my appreciation. Drive safely, Michelle."

He disappeared from the kitchen before she could respond and within seconds she heard him go outside through the back door.

Like an automaton, she cleaned and did everything she could to anticipate his needs before driving away from the condo. The time she'd spent taking care of him had brought her indescribable joy. She couldn't comprehend a permanent cessation of so much happiness.

Two hours later she pulled up in the driveway of her house in Riverside. During the drive she'd made the decision to approach her brother in private. If he was shocked by what she had to ask him, she'd know it instantly. At least that way he could break it to Sherilyn in his own time.

At lunch time on Wednesday, she finally found the temerity to enter the law firm where Graham ran his practice with two other attorneys. When Michelle told the receptionist she was there to see her brother, she learned he was still in conference. She would have to wait.

That's all she'd been doing since Sunday night. Waiting for this moment that would decide her future… By now she was sick to her stomach with fear.

"Michelle?"

She was so jumpy, she almost fell out of the chair getting up. "Hi, Graham. I hope you don't mind my dropping by like this."

"Why would I mind? Sherilyn and I have wondered why you haven't been by the house since you came home on Sunday." The worried look in his eyes made the pit in her stomach worse. "Come on in and let's talk."

She walked in his office and sat down. Instead of going behind his desk, he sat down next to her.

"I recognize an anguished look on your face when I see one. Tell me what's wrong."

Her mouth had gone dry. "Coming to you about this is probably the hardest thing I've ever had to do in my life."

Graham's expression grew solemn. "Harder than having to face the fact that Rob wasn't going to get better?"

"In a way, yes. Death is a natural process of life in the scheme of things. What I'm struggling with *isn't* natural. That's why I came to talk to you in private."

Part of her wanted to run, but another part knew she had to see this through. "I know you share everything with Sherilyn. However once you hear what I have to say, you may decide otherwise."

Her brother didn't flinch. "Go on."

"I need to ask you a question. It's absolutely vital you be honest with me when you answer it."

"Have you ever known me not to be?"

"No." Her fingers clutched the armrests of the chair. "How would you feel if Zak told you he was in love with Lynette?"

"He's already told us his feelings on that score, but if he hadn't, it would stretch my imagination beyond its bounds," he answered immediately.

She felt the blood drain out of her face. "That's all I wanted to know," she whispered. "Thanks, Graham."

Somehow she got out of the chair, but her body was weaving. "Easy," he murmured, putting firm hands on her shoulders to force her back down.

"You haven't asked me *why*," he said.

She kept her eyes averted. "I *know* why."

"Then what's the reason for this visit?"

"I shouldn't have come."

"Why don't you ask me how I'd feel if Zak told me he was in love with *you?*"

The blood rushed to her ears.

''Now's your chance. Go ahead. I can assure you the answer would be different.''

''I don't see how it could be different. The same rules apply,'' her voice throbbed.

''Rules? I thought you were talking about love.''

''We're all family, Graham.''

''True.''

''But if he and Lynette did love each other, would you give them your blessing?''

''Yes, but as I said a minute ago, it would stretch the imagination because he's always been crazy about someone else in this family.''

She could hardly breathe.

''H-how do you know that?''

''Michelle...'' Graham reached out to shake her arm gently. ''Surely you don't need me to tell you. The night he heard you and Rob were engaged, something died inside Zak.''

She moaned.

''He'd been so busy trying to be worthy of you, he thought he had more time. Sherilyn and I despaired of his ever really being happy again.

''That is...until a few weeks ago when I came home from the pharmacy with his medicine. The look in his eyes when he told me you had agreed to be his nurse terrified me because I knew what that look was all about.''

Graham got to his feet and pulled her with him. He stared at her for a long time. ''Are you in love with him?''

''Yes.'' Tears spilled from her eyes. ''I didn't think I could fall in love again. But then Zak came to the funeral and was so understanding...I felt guilty because it was too soon to be thinking about another man, especially my sister-in-law's brother. That's why I've avoided him for the last couple of years.''

A strange sound came out of Graham. ''Has he spoken about his feelings now?''

''Yes.''

''Did you turn him down because you felt Sherilyn and I wouldn't approve?''

''That's part of it—'' she cried out in agony. ''When he asked me to think about it, I told him he deserved a young wife who could give him babies.''

Graham looked wounded. ''He wants *you*, Michelle.''

''Mike Francis helped me to realize that. He explained a lot of things that taught me where Zak has been coming from.''

''Is that where you went Saturday afternoon?''

''Yes.''

Her brother groaned. ''It's all making sense.''

''What do you mean?''

''Zak was so restless, he wanted to go back to Carlsbad Saturday evening. So he phoned Gail's house to find out how long you were going to be. The next thing Sherilyn and I knew, he'd gone to bed. On Sunday morning that picture of you in Mike's arms leaped off the sports page.''

Michelle buried her face in her hands. ''All I do is hurt him.''

''So what are you going to do about it?''

She wiped her eyes. ''I'm going to drive to Carlsbad and take care of him for the rest of the week whether he likes it or not.

''The thing is, after we got back to the condo on

Sunday, he told me he didn't need a nurse any longer. I knew he meant business when I received a generous check in the mail from him yesterday afternoon.

"He's really written me off, Graham. I'm afraid he's under the impression that I can't get past my feelings for Rob. And even if I could, I'd want an older man."

Her brother's jaw hardened. "But you're going to let him know otherwise, right?"

"If he'll give me the chance," her voice shook. "The problem is, I left his spare key on the kitchen counter at the condo. He might refuse to let me in."

Graham pulled the key ring from his pocket. "Here." He handed her his key. "You have my permission to break and enter. Do whatever it takes to put his heart back together."

She threw her arms around her brother. After a long bone-crushing hug, he let her go. Michelle left his office clutching the key in her hand.

A thrill of excitement mingled with fear raced through her body at the prospect of seeing Zak again. She hurried back to her house to get packed, not wanting to waste another precious second away from him.

It was half past four before she turned into the alley. Since she didn't have the remote, she drove to the visitor parking at the end of the cul-de-sac. Grabbing her suitcase and the sack of groceries she'd bought, she rushed toward the back entrance and let herself in the condo.

"Zak?" she called out to let him know it wasn't an intruder who'd broken in. When there was no answer, she cried his name again. Still no response.

Gathering her courage, she headed for his bedroom. No sign of him in there or the bathroom. A couple of shirts and sweats lay on the end of his unmade bed. A towel had been dropped on the floor.

She went to her bedroom to deposit her suitcase, then hurried into the kitchen to put the groceries away. Two empty pizza cartons and plastic salad containers sat on the counter, evidence of what he'd been eating for meals.

No doubt he was out taking a walk. She set about quickly to get a meal started. When she opened the fridge, she discovered he'd never eaten the sandwiches she'd made for him.

After cleaning the kitchen, she put in a CD of some Frank Sinatra favorites, then opened the living room curtains and sliding door to let in the ocean breeze.

With the music playing, she hurried into his bathroom to scour it and put clean sheets on his bed. When everything was done, she started a wash in the laundry room.

Seven o'clock rolled around and he still hadn't come back. Maybe he wasn't out on the beach after all. It was possible he'd driven somewhere in his truck against doctor's orders.

Sure enough when she looked in the garage, it was empty.

She ate alone, then put the food away to warm up later when he came in. At midnight she closed the glass door and pulled the curtains.

Heartsick, she lay down on the couch and watched TV. He had to come in at some point. The next thing she knew she was awakened by the sounds of the mid-morning news blaring in her ears.

Michelle jumped up off the couch and hurried into Zak's bedroom. He'd never come home!

She phoned the family on her cell to find out if they knew where he might be. Sherilyn said the last time they'd spoken to him was Tuesday evening. By the time they'd concluded their conversation, Michelle agreed with her sister-in-law that Zak must have slept over at a friend's.

After promising to keep in touch, Michelle called his office on the hunch that he'd decided to go back to work. Doug answered and told her neither he or Miki had seen Zak, only talked to him on the phone. As far as they knew, the boss wouldn't be in until next week.

By the time they said goodbye, she was panicked. Maybe he'd driven himself to the doctor's office yesterday because he had trouble breathing. He could be in the hospital right now!

With trembling hands she looked up the number in the directory and phoned Dr. Tebbs. When she told the receptionist her fears, the other woman put her on hold, then came back on the phone a few minutes later with the news that the doctor hadn't seen Zak since his last appointment.

Relief swamped her system. After promising the receptionist that Zak would be there on Friday, Michelle hung up wondering where on earth he'd gone.

Because she'd exhausted every possibility she could think of, there was nothing she could do but keep busy until he walked in.

Afraid she might miss him if she went out on the deck, she settled down in the living room with a new mystery she'd bought. It held her interest for all of ten minutes, then she put it down. This was agony.

She headed for the kitchen to get herself a drink. As she was reaching for a cola from the fridge, she heard the sound of the garage door opening. Thank heaven! It was after two. She'd thought he was never going to come back.

The fear that he'd be angry she'd invaded his condo without his knowledge caused her heart to pound wildly in her chest.

It was too late to admit that she should have phoned him on his cell yesterday. She could have saved herself hours of suffering. But she'd wanted to surprise him. Now she found herself regretting that impulse.

To her chagrin she could hear Zak talking to someone. He wasn't alone!

She clutched the edge of the counter top, not knowing what to expect. The likelihood he'd seen her car at the end of the cul-de-sac was remote. If he'd brought home a girlfriend, Michelle was going to come as a big shock in more ways than one.

Instead the shock was hers.

Two black-haired men of the same height and powerful build entered the living room wearing lightweight business suits. They looked incredibly alike from their bone structure down to their rugged jawlines with those five o'clock shadows.

Stunned, Michelle put a hand to her mouth to stifle her cry, but Zak must have heard her because his head jerked around in her direction.

The other man looked to see what Zak was seeing, and removed his sunglasses. His black eyes found their target. From a few yards away the only other obvious difference between him and his hazel-eyed son was about twenty-five years.

Michelle had always suspected Zak had some Greek heritage. Now she knew he did. Standing next to his father who possessed a more olive complexion and thicker brows, they looked to be business men from a prosperous family like the kind you would expect to see walking along the streets of Athens.

Zak acted as if it were perfectly normal to find her standing there in his kitchen with a can of soda in her hands. After the painful way they'd parted on Sunday night, she could only admire his aplomb.

Without missing a beat he said, "Michelle? Let me introduce you to my father, Nicholas Zannis from New York City. Nick? This is my brother-in-law's sister, Michelle Howard. She's the nurse who's been looking after me since my accident."

"How do you do, Mr. Zannis."

For Zak to have brought his father to the condo meant that whatever he'd learned about his beginnings, the knowledge had at least managed to take the sword out of his hand.

Nick moved closer. They shook hands over the counter. He stared at her in that intense way Zak did. "My son says you've taken impeccable care of him. I'm particularly glad of it because I've been searching for him twenty-five years now."

"All this time?" she half-gasped the words.

"It's a long story." Up close his eyes held a sadness, a melancholy that tugged at her heart.

Her gaze darted to Zak's. His expression was harder to read. What was he thinking right now? This man was his flesh and blood father. She'd give anything to know if Zak was happy, or in pain.

"Are either of you hungry? I've made a lot of food. All I have to do is warm it up."

"That's very thoughtful of you," his father said,

"but I have to be back in New York tonight. Zak was kind enough to let me see his home on my way to the airport."

"You're leaving already?" All Michelle could seem to do was exclaim with one question after the other.

"Zak has important business he must take care of since his accident. So do I. As soon as his passport comes, we'll vacation in Greece where he'll meet the family."

"I see."

Nicholas Zannis had an aura of confidence and authority about him. Clearly he was a man who was used to being in charge. Zak had inherited those traits. Already his father acted like Zak had always been a part of him. It was so strange, and yet so natural, too.

Michelle couldn't help but wonder how all this was going to affect the family. Of course they'd be happy for him, but just seeing Zak with his birthfather was like he'd suddenly become someone else with a whole new identity.

"While Zak shows you his condo, do you mind if I take a picture of both of you?" She hoped it was all right with Zak.

He turned to his son. "Can you stand to pose one more time with me?"

"Why not," Zak murmured.

"I'll just dash in the bedroom for my camera."

When she came out again carrying her instamatic, Nick happened to be remarking on the excellent workmanship of the coffee table. "The Zannis corporation owns many companies. One of them is an export business for textiles and furniture items from Greece to the States and elsewhere, but I've seen nothing this fine."

He lifted his dark head where she could see slivers of silver among the black near his temples. ''Who crafted this?''

''Zak made it in his spare time,'' Michelle volunteered with pride.

His father appeared visibly impressed and patted Zak's shoulder. He turned to Michelle.

''Would you take a picture of us standing next to my son's masterpiece? His grandfather Theo will be overjoyed to learn that one of his grandchildren has inherited his love of working with wood.''

Zak couldn't help but be thrilled his father had praised his remarkable skill without realizing it. Michelle was still reeling from the fact that Zak had a whole other family anxious to meet him—a family ready to welcome him with open arms.

This was going to be much harder on Sherilyn than Michelle had first supposed. That was because she hadn't yet met Zak's dynamic father.

''I'll follow you around and use up the rest of the film. We'll get double prints made so he can send them to you.'' After years of speculation about Zak's origins, the family would be anxious for copies, too.

She tried to be unobtrusive while Zak gave him the tour. Eventually the men went out on the deck and walked along the beach for a few minutes. Michelle stayed behind to watch them from the living room.

If this situation was surreal to Michelle, she couldn't even imagine Zak's frame of mind by now. His real father was standing there in front of his condo talking to him.

Whatever the explanation for their separation, it hit Michelle that if father and son had always been together, Zak would have grown up in New York. Michelle would never have known him. There'd have been no Zak in her life.

She couldn't comprehend it. If she tried, it made her ill.

"This is the hard part," she heard his father say in a voice laced with emotion. They'd just come back in the living room. "You have my phone numbers and addresses. I have yours. We'll see each other soon."

"I promise."

Zak never made a promise he didn't keep. Already his life had changed in profound ways.

His father kissed him on both cheeks before turning to Michelle. "It was a pleasure to meet you. I hope to see you again. Now I have to be going."

"Zak shouldn't be driving yet," she blurted, uncaring if Zak didn't like her interference. "I'd be happy to run you to the airport."

"Thank you, but I rented a car when I flew in yesterday morning. It's in the garage." He turned to Zak. "If you'd walk me out."

"Of course."

It was obvious Zak's father wanted their last words to be in private. After knowing Zak since he was nine years old, it gave her the oddest feeling to be relegated to outsider status, looking in.

Without conscious thought she retraced their steps to the beach in an effort to deal with her own chaotic emotions.

Since coming back to Carlsbad, she'd been bursting inside with the love she had to shower on Zak, only to discover his time and thoughts had been tied up with the man who'd been absent from his life all these years.

Distracted for a moment by the sound of a motor, she turned her head in time to see a Jeep crawling alongside her. The cute, dark-blond lifeguard she'd noticed driving by before smiled at her.

"How's it going?"

"Good."

"I always see you out here alone."

"I'm a nurse taking care of a patient who's been bedridden."

The jeep came to a full stop. He climbed out. The guy couldn't be a day over twenty-three. She had to admit he was good looking. Lynette should be here, she thought!

"So when do you go off duty?"

With so many young, beautiful California girls looking for fun along the miles of surf, she couldn't believe he was making a pass at her.

"*She doesn't,*" a vibrant male voice answered before she could.

Zak seemed to have materialized out of nowhere. Her heart turned over.

Though the lifeguard was in great shape, he was no match for Zak who regarded him like a bug under a microscope. His hands had gone to hips. In his business suit and tie he had an intimidating presence the younger man couldn't help but be aware of.

"Hadn't you better be looking for swimmers in trouble while you're still on duty?"

The lifeguard scowled. "Who asked you to butt in?"

"I'm her patient."

"Sure. Whatever." He climbed back in his Jeep and flipped Zak off before resuming his tour of the beach.

"That wasn't necessary, Zak."

"He's been checking you out for the last couple of weeks. It's time he poached somewhere else."

Nothing ever slipped past Zak, not even from his sick bed. Right now his male scrutiny was making her nervous.

She rubbed damp palms against the sides of her white cotton pants, hardly knowing where to begin. "I'm so sorry for the shock I gave you earlier. To have intruded on your privacy when you needed this time alone with your father—Please forgive me, Zak."

"Why did you come?"

Her heart groaned at his withering tone. "I couldn't rest worrying about you here alone when I knew the doctor hadn't given you a clean bill of health yet. But I was afraid you wouldn't let me come if I phoned you, so I asked Graham for his key."

Her hands unconsciously made an arc in front of her. "Please don't blame him. He gave it to me because he and Sherilyn are anxious about you, too," she spoke faster because he wasn't saying anything.

"It doesn't happen often, but sometimes the lung collapses again. We'd all feel better if I stayed with you for a while longer, as a precaution."

What she'd just told him was a portion of the truth, but this wasn't the moment to bare her soul to him. He was putting on a good front, but the father he'd wondered about all his life had just left the condo. Zak had to be grappling with so many feelings and emotions, there was only so much he could process.

It hadn't been that long since his hospital stay. She could see physical signs that he was more drained than he knew.

"When did you get here?"

At least he hadn't ordered off his property yet. She could be grateful for that much. "Late yesterday afternoon."

The enigmatic expression in his eyes told her little. "I phoned Mr. Jamison on Monday morning. He arranged for a meeting between my father and me. It took place yesterday afternoon. I drove to Los Angeles and checked into a motel to break up the drive."

"So *that's* where you were."

"Little did I know I'd end up with him following me home today." He stared at her through shuttered eyes. "I'd left the place in a mess. I suppose it's fortunate you showed up without invitation and made it spotless once more."

"I'm glad I was good for something," she said in a shaky voice. "Zak? Let's go in the house so you can lie down. You look…pale."

"I'm all right." But she noticed he turned and started walking toward the condo without argument.

"All the way to your bedroom," she ordered once they'd reached the living room.

After locking the sliding door, she hurried after him to help him off with his jacket and shirt. He went into the bathroom and came out a few minutes later in pajama bottoms.

Michelle had turned down the covers. When he got in bed she heard his sigh of exhaustion. He was emotionally and physically spent.

She covered him to the waist and took his vital signs. Except for his pulse which was a trifle fast, everything else appeared to be normal. She felt his forehead. He was a little warm. However she wasn't too alarmed until she looked in his eyes.

The irises had turned more gray than green, a sign of emotional turmoil in Zak's case. "What can I bring you?" she inquired urgently.

A haunted look had crept over his handsome face. It aged his appearance.

"Forgetfulness."

She sank down next to him. "What do you mean?"

"I knew it would be a risk to let my curiosity get the better of me."

"And now you wish it hadn't?" she whispered.

"Dear God, Michelle—" His eyes closed tightly. "My mother was murdered."

The revelation was so horrific, only one instinct drove her now.

She stretched out beside his body and wrapped her arms around him. With a deep moan, Zak turned toward her seeking a more comfortable position. Once he'd buried his face in her neck, they clung.

CHAPTER NINE

"MY PARENTS were on vacation when it happened," Zak began. "They spent a night at the Disneyland Hotel on their way to the beach. I was three years old and scared of everything except the train.

"They'd just finished dinner. My mother told my father she'd take me for one more ride around, then join him in the room."

Zak took a shuddering breath. "My father waved us off and returned to the hotel. He never saw us again."

There was no earthly comfort for a tragedy of this magnitude. All Michelle could do was kiss the dampened black tendrils near his temple, desperate to share his pain with him.

"A year later the police in San Bernadino contacted the FBI. A woman's body had been found in a shallow grave in the foothills. With the help of dental records, she was identified as my mother, Carolyn Zannis, but there was no child buried with her.

"Forensics revealed she'd been the victim of a violent crime. Many exhaustive searches were made for me, to no avail. The police lieutenant leading the investigation theorized it had probably started out as a kidnapping for a ransom that had gone wrong. Apparently my father's family is very affluent.

"They used their money and considerable influence to look for me. The police felt my chances of being alive were virtually nonexistent, but because my body was never found, my father never gave up hope.''

"That poor man. The suffering he's been through.'' she whispered heartbrokenly, hugging Zak tighter.

"Two years ago a break came in the case when a man who was shot by the woman he tried to kidnap in Oregon was taken into custody. Before he died, he confessed to killing other women in Oregon and California. It turns out my mother was one of them.''

Michelle groaned. "Did the man say anything about you?''

"No. But a search of the van he'd been living in gave clues that helped the police trace his history. It seems he was married and held a job at a pet store in Rancho Cucamonga at the time of my mother's death.

"The person who owned the trailer park where they lived remembered that they'd adopted a little dark-haired boy and lived there with him and a pet poodle for about a year. Then they moved on because of a better job somewhere else.

"According to him, they were nice church going people who named their son Zakariah from the Bible. The trailer park owner made a positive identification from the pictures the investigator showed him.''

"I don't believe it," she cried softly, "but I have to.''

"Apparently they decided to sell me to a couple in Riverside.''

Her breath caught. "Riverside—''

"Ironic isn't it?'' he muttered. "The new couple were adamant about wanting a white child. They were willing to pay good money through illegal means. I lived with them until they were killed in a car accident on the freeway which I survived because of my seat belt.

"After a stay in the hospital I was sent to live with a family designated by the state to provide temporary emergency care for children in my situation. From the age of five to six I lived with three sets of foster parents.

"The saga ended when the Sadlers adopted me. The police are still searching for the woman who was married to my mother's killer."

Michelle pressed her forehead against his. "Your father never gave up looking for you, Zak."

"No."

As soon as Zak could get past this new grief about his mother, the knowledge that he was loved by both his birthparents would sink deep in his heart and bring him peace.

"Just think what finding you has meant to your father. Tell me about your parents."

"On my mother's side I have an aunt, cousins and grandparents. My mother was a green-eyed, dark blond woman of Scotch-Irish descent.

"My father married again, a Greek woman named Anna. I have a stepbrother Paul who's twenty-four, and a stepsister Christine who's twenty-two. I forget how many cousins.

"The extended family both in New York and Greece are close knit. They all work in the business tog—"

Michelle's cell phone went off, interrupting them.

"I'm sure that's Sherilyn and Graham wondering where you are."

She eased out of his arms when it was the last thing she wanted to do. Her phone was in her pocket.

"It's Sherilyn," she said after checking the caller ID. "What would you like me to do?"

"I'll talk to her."

Michelle handed him the phone. "I'm going to warm up dinner for us."

She'd only been in the kitchen a few minutes when Zak appeared. "That was quick," she murmured.

At a glance she could tell he wasn't as drawn as before. "I explained I'd been to see my father and wanted to tell them about it. They'll be here by eight and are planning to stay over."

Disappointment pierced Michelle like a metal shaft.

She'd counted on being alone with Zak tonight. After so many years of hiding her feelings, she thought she couldn't stand it any longer if she couldn't tell him she loved him and wanted to marry him.

But right now he had a pressing need to discuss everything with Sherilyn and Graham. For the time being she understood his mind and heart were involved elsewhere. Until they left tomorrow, she would have to remain silent.

"I'm sure they can't think about anything else." Her thoughts flew ahead. "In a few minutes the manicotti will be ready. I think I'll use the time to make up the bed in the study for them."

"While you do that I'll get my suitcase out of the truck. My father gave me the baby book and photo album my mother made."

The mention of such irreplaceable treasures brought a sheen of moisture to her eyes.

He paused midstride. "Did I tell you he's asked me to think about moving my company to the East Coast to become part of the Zannis Corporation?"

While she staggered from the unexpected revelation, he disappeared down the hall.

Fear of a different kind crept through her. In a twinkling of an eye, Zak's world had changed forever.

He had a father who loved him and wanted him with him. He was a favorite son who'd been lost and now was found. His father had embraced him with open arms. He was urging Zak to take his rightful place in the family.

What could be more natural for a father who'd grieved for his long lost little boy than to want to shower the grown man with all the blessings entitled by his birthright?

Zak wouldn't be human if he didn't want to live out the rest of his life as a Zannis. They were his people, his genes. From the little she'd gleaned so far, his was a great heritage. A whole new world was about to manifest itself.

Who knew what opportunities awaited him? In the privileged Zannis circle of friends, there might be a young beautiful Greek woman who would set his heart on fire the minute he met her. They would have beautiful children together. He would never grow tired of her or leave her.

The more she thought about it, the more she was convinced that all along life had been holding something else in store for Zak. It would explain the reason why he'd never found the right woman to marry.

Two years have passed since the last time we saw each other, Michelle. I'm letting you know I'm finally all grown up.

Those words seemed to have conjured his father, leading Michelle to conclude that his sudden dramatic

appearance on the scene had been anything but a co-
incidence.

Like the sealing of pharoah's tomb which no earthly
hand could prevent once the great stones thundered into
place, the main chapter in Zak's life had started unfolding with a momentum too great to hold back.

The message was clear. The first twenty-eight years
of his life had been a prologue. Zak was meant to explore his new world free of any encumbrance.

With hindsight she could see that she'd already followed her own destiny by marrying Rob. Everything
had turned out the way it was supposed to have happened.

There would be no marriage between her and Zak.

You didn't put new wine in an old bottle or it would
burst. New wine was meant for a new bottle so both
were preserved.

The saying she'd heard all her life made more sense
than ever.

Maybe the realization that the situation with Zak had
always been out of her hands was the reason she was
able to carry on in front of him before the family arrived
as if nothing momentous had occurred.

When she met her brother at the door, she knew he
was expecting to see her aglow with happiness. Yet all
Graham had to do was glance at her closed expression
and the light faded from his eyes.

Sherilyn and Lynette were right behind him. Michelle
hugged both of them, unable to tell what her sister-in-
law was thinking.

They walked on through to the front of the condo
where Zak was waiting. He'd put the albums and en-

velopes of pictures on the coffee table for the family to see.

There was an emotionally-charged atmosphere in the living room as everyone sat down and Zak began talking about his mother's murder. Except for a comment here and there, Michelle remained in the background while the rest of them tried to recover from their horror. In time they started asking questions.

He showed them photographs. Pictures didn't lie. The baby book told of a loving beginning with extraordinary parents from an extraordinary, prominent family.

What emerged over the next three hours was the inescapable fact that Zak was Nicholas Zannis's beloved flesh and blood. He wanted his son to live near him and become a part of him in every sense of the word.

From here on out it was clear to one and all that no matter Zak's decision down the road, there would always be another person in his life who had a hold on his heart, a person whose pain had been infinite, a man who had every right to want catch up on those years of fatherhood stolen from him in the most cruel of ways imaginable.

Zak needed time with his father, too. He needed to bask in the knowledge that he hadn't been abandoned.

All those talks along the beach when he'd been a young teenager came flooding back to Michelle. The anguish he'd felt, his inability to trust Graham for fear getting close to him might be temporary, too. But Graham had proved his love for Zak so totally, he'd won him over.

Michelle looked down at the floor. Her heart went out to her brother and sister-in law who had to be filled with a dichotomy of emotions right now.

What had taken them years to accomplish, Nicholas Zannis had achieved within one day by simply appearing in Zak's life and telling him he'd never stopped loving him or looking for him.

What son could be immune to that kind of testimony?

She knew it was the question foremost in all their minds.

As for Zak, he'd had a day and a night to absorb the tragic details of his mother's death and could now look ahead to a bright new future in a family where he belonged by right of birth.

She could only imagine the joy and excitement kindling beneath the surface at the possibilities. Judging by the speculative look in Graham's eyes, he was thinking the same thing about his wife's brother.

Michelle couldn't bring herself to glance at Sherilyn who adored Zak. In her own way she'd grieved since the day he'd told the family he wanted to live in Carlsbad. Sherilyn had never said the words, but Michelle had a hunch her sister-in-law felt like she'd failed her adopted brother in some way.

Nothing could be further from the truth. Zak had always loved the ocean. He'd chosen a place that wasn't too far from Riverside so he could have as much contact with them as possible, but human nature had a tendency to be paranoid.

"Greek women are really beautiful," Lynette observed in a small voice. She'd been studying the pictures for a long time. "Your stepsister is gorgeous."

Michelle's breath caught because she'd had the exact same thoughts. Like everyone else, her poor niece was battling conflicted feelings that swirled beneath the surface, too.

"She's not any more attractive than you."

Lynette flashed Zak a wry smile. "Nice try, Uncle Zak."

"I said it because it's true," he asserted with intimidating authority.

"How soon are you going to New York?" Sherilyn's question had been the one Michelle was afraid to ask.

"I'll apply for a passport tomorrow after Michelle drives me to the doctor."

"Do they take a long time to process?"

Zak's disturbing gaze leveled on Michelle. "What do you think?"

"Mine came within two weeks. By the time you're completely healed, your passport could easily be here. Under the circumstances I'll return to Riverside and get ready for my new nursing job."

Graham eyed her with a grim expression. "Do you have one lined up already?"

"Yes," she lied.

Forgive me, Graham. I'll explain everything later. Once you hear what I have to say, you'll understand.

Zak studied her through veiled eyes. "When did this happen?

"I checked in with home nursing services a couple of days ago."

Before he could ask any more questions his cell phone rang.

"I'll get it," she volunteered. She was seated closest to the kitchen where he'd left it on the counter.

Sherilyn frowned. "Who'd be calling you after midnight knowing you've been ill?"

Michelle handed it to him, careful not to brush his fingers.

"It's my father. I asked him to phone and let me know he'd arrived safely in New York. Excuse me for a moment." Zak left the room.

After he'd gone, Graham got up from his chair. "I think it's time we all turned in." He gave Michelle a pained glance that said they'd talk in the morning.

She turned to Lynette. "You can sleep in the room I've been using. I put clean sheets on the bed before you came."

"Where are you going to sleep?"

"Tonight will probably be my last night here. I'm going to stay out on the deck lounger so I can enjoy the ocean. Who knows when I'll see it again."

"Can I sleep out there on the other one with you?"

"Sure." She hugged her niece.

"I love the ocean at night."

"So do I."

Lynette needed comfort so badly she was even willing to turn to her Aunt Michelle whom she'd been avoiding for the last few weeks. Little did her niece know Michelle craved the company of someone dear and familiar, too.

They all needed each other if they were going to get through this night in one piece. Thank heaven Graham and Sherilyn had each other to cling to.

It didn't take long to get ready for bed. Michelle and Lynette put on T-shirts and shorts. While Zak was still in his room with the door shut, everyone said good night.

After Michelle turned out all the lights, she joined Lynette on the deck where they'd carried pillows and blankets.

Once they were settled, Lynette turned on her side

toward Michelle. "I have a feeling Uncle Zak's going to move away forever. It'll kill Mom and Dad," she whispered.

Michelle swallowed hard. "Even if he does, you know he'll make every effort to come home and see all of you." She tried to infuse enthusiasm in her voice. "Just think of the exciting trips to New York."

"It's never going to be the same again. You can tell me I'm awful for saying this, but I wish his father had never found him."

"You're not awful, Lynette. I think there's a selfish part in all of us that would like to pretend this was all a bad dream."

"That's what it's like. Zak has changed."

"In what way?"

"I don't know exactly. He just seems different. Older."

"The news about his mother was chilling."

"I don't want to think about it. I can't get over how much he resembles his father. From those photos, he fits right in with all of them, but he's by far the best looking."

"I thought his stepbrother was handsome."

"He is, but Zak looks like a Greek god."

"You're right."

A sigh escaped. "Zak has always stood out."

"Now that we know his background, it's easy to see why."

"You wouldn't think heritage would make such a difference, but it does."

"In some ways. In others, he's a Sadler."

"I'm afraid his Zannis side is going to take over. They have their own corporate jet and a villa on one of the Greek islands. With their millions, Uncle Zak wouldn't need to work.''

''Everyone needs work, and money would never sway your uncle. But the opportunity to get to know his father is another story. Under the circumstances, I'm glad you haven't moved out of your parents' house yet. If Zak does relocate to the east coast, they're going to be so thankful you're there for a little while longer anyway.''

''On the drive here, Mom talked about going back to teaching school next year. It will feel different if she does.''

The fallout from Zak's news had left no one unscathed.

''That's a while away yet. What time do you have to be to work tomorrow?''

''Two to nine. Since I'm not taking classes this semester, that's my schedule for the month.''

''Do you like your job?''

''It's okay, but I plan to quit after New Years and get back in school.'' That was the only good news to come out of their conversation. ''Thanks for talking to me, Aunt Michelle.'' She sounded sleepy.

''I was just going to tell you the same thing. Good night, honey.''

''G'night.''

With a throbbing ache in her heart, Michelle turned on her other side and concentrated on the crash of the surf to bring oblivion for a short while. Anything to blot out the pain.

''Michelle?''

She heard her name being called. Thinking it was

Lynette who wanted to tell her something else, she twisted around.

"Michelle—wake up."

It suddenly dawned on her it was a man's voice. She opened her eyes to discover Zak hunkered down next to her. He put a finger to her lips so she wouldn't cry out. The fog had rolled in, making it impossible for her to gauge the exact time.

"I just came back from a walk. Will you check my vital signs? If there are any surprises, I want to know about them before I see the doctor this morning."

It was morning already?

She raised up. Zak removed the blanket and helped her to her feet. Their bodies brushed against each other. In her sleep induced state, it felt like the most natural thing in the world for his hand to span the back of her neck to guide her past Lynette who was out for the count.

When they reached his bedroom, he shut the door without making a sound.

"Sit down on the side of the bed and we'll get started," she whispered, reaching for the blood pressure cup and stethoscope in a kind of daze. He removed his hooded sweatshirt and tossed it to the far side of the bed.

By the time she'd given him a thorough examination, she was wide awake and terrified to stay in his room a moment longer.

In a tremulous voice she said, "As far as I can tell, you're as good as new."

"That's a relief." His hands shot to her hips. He pulled her between his legs covered by his sweats. "Now I want to hear the news I've been waiting for."

He'd brought her so close, she had to put her hands on his shoulders to prevent herself from falling against him.

Refusing to look at him she said, "What news is that?"

His hands tightened. "Don't start playing games with me. We're both adults. I've given you time to think about my proposal. What's your answer?"

Hardening her heart she said, "Don't you think you'd know what it was by now if it were yes?"

Shadows darkened his face. "Twelve hours ago we held each other on this bed. If the phone hadn't rung, we would never have left it."

"You're wrong, Zak." She tried to back away from him, but she was no match for his strength.

"Did I just imagine the kisses you gave me while the tears ran down your cheeks?" he demanded in a voice of ice.

"No. Of course not. I was trying to comfort you in the only way I knew how."

"You mean like you used to do when I was a troubled child?"

"Yes."

"What about the kiss you gave me while we were dancing?" he bit out. "In case you don't remember it, let me refresh your memory."

His mouth closed over hers with smothering force. No longer hampered in his movements, Zak lay back against the mattress, pulling her on top of him.

The savagery of his kiss took her breath. He crushed her in his arms.

"Zak—" she cried, but that was as far as she got

because he'd rolled her over so she lay beneath him. His strong, powerful legs engulfed hers.

"I've wanted you forever, and you want me," came his impassioned murmur before he began seducing her with his mouth. Slowly, inexorably, his long, deep, sensuous kisses drew the response she couldn't hold back any longer.

She had no concept of time while they clung to each other in a wine dark rapture. No experience in life had prepared her for this burning desire.

His hands tangled in her silky hair. "I'm in love with you, darling," he whispered on a ragged breath as his lips roved over her face, bringing her body to a feverish pitch of need only he could assuage.

Those intense green eyes of his stared into hers. "You're the most beautiful thing in my life. You always have been. We were meant to be together."

Every part of his being was crying out to her. She had to stop this before things went any farther.

"Zak—" She lifted her hands to his face to prevent him from kissing her again. "A few days ago I'd reached the point where I was beginning to believe that was true. But—"

"But nothing!" he cut in fiercely. "Don't you dare tell me that because I've suddenly found out I have a father who's alive, everything has changed."

Her head moved from side to side in despair. "Deny it all you want, but it *does* change things. You just don't know it yet."

His lips twisted unpleasantly. "And you do?"

"Yes," she cried. "He's asked you to fly to Greece with him the minute your passport comes through. A father who loves his son has plans for him. He can't wait to show you off!

"He'll want to introduce you to the rest of the family, to his friends." She took a shuddering breath. "You'll meet your own kind of people."

"*My* kind of people?" His eyes glittered dangerously. "I thought I'd been living around my own kind of people since my sister married your brother."

She tried to sit up, but his chest prevented her from moving. "I didn't mean that the way it sounded. It came out wrong."

"Then explain it to me."

"I-it's possible you'll meet an exciting younger woman while you're there," she stammered.

His eyes darkened until she couldn't see the green. "I meet entertaining women of different ages all the time right here in Carlsbad. What does that have to do with anything?"

"You've purposely misunderstood my meaning. The women you'll meet there are the kind of whom your father will approve."

"It's Graham's approval I care about. What else is on your mind?"

"You're not giving yourself a chance to find out what life has in store for you. You have no baggage to hinder you if you decide you want to...move back East."

To her shock, he got up from the bed and stood there looking down at her with such a wintry expression, it frightened her.

"Where in the hell did you get the idea that I'd ever leave California?"

She struggled to get up, and made it as far as the side

of the bed. "It would be understandable if you wanted to, Zak. Your family—"

"My family is here," he ground out.

"I realize that, but you have another family in New York. You're only twenty-eight. Your father is still young. The two of you have years of life ahead to get to know each other the way a father and son should."

His hands went to his hips in a forbidding stance. "In case it escaped your notice, Graham has done the job since I was nine. I intend to stay around and enjoy our relationship until one of us dies."

Michelle slid off the bed to face him. "Why are you being like this, Zak?" Her blue eyes implored him. "When you were a boy, you cried to me because your birthparents had abandoned you. You couldn't understand why they had left you.

"Now a miracle has happened and you've found out you had adoring parents after all. You have a father who wants to make up for everything you both lost. He has the means and the desire to give you what is rightfully yours."

He shook his head. "You think because we've found each other, it wipes out the years of life and loving I've known with my sister and Graham?

"Is it possible you believe I can just walk away from them as if none of the last twenty years ever mattered?" His voice throbbed with emotion.

"Maybe you have to be in my shoes to understand. So let me make it clear to you one more time. Although Sherilyn is only my sister, she took care of me like a mother after our parents died. I realize I had a loving birthmother, but she didn't raise me. My sister did. I love her.

"As for Graham, he reached out and taught me to trust. He's been father and brother all rolled into one. I could have searched the earth over and never found his equal. I love, respect and honor him in every way."

His chest heaved. "I'm sure my stepbrother and sister feel the same way about Nick. The point is, he and the woman he married raised them, not me.

"Of course I'm going to make the effort to get to know him. He seems to be a wonderful man. I'm excited to meet my relatives on both sides. From the pictures I've seen, my mother and her sister bear a strong resemblance to each other. That makes her more real to me as a result.

"But make no mistake—my heart is here, Michelle. I'm one hundred percent Sadler and proud of it."

She couldn't prevent the tears dropping hard and fast.

"Forgive me for making assumptions, Zak. I never meant you to think I didn't believe you loved Sherilyn and Graham."

He rubbed the back of his neck. "You and I go back a long way, Michelle. During those earliest years you got stuck with all my pain and insecurities. It makes perfect sense that you internalized everything I told you. In the process of growing up I moved past my hangups, but it appears you didn't.

"At this point the only question of any relevance to me is, are you stuck in the past because you loved Rob too much?

"I know you're physically attracted to me. What we shared on the bed a few minutes ago is proof of that.

"Yet physical attraction is only one part of a relationship. I found out through trial and error that if it's the only part, then it's doomed not to last. But apparently it was all there for you and Rob,'' his voice grated.

"I didn't want to believe it. I went into total denial. I couldn't face the fact you'd fallen in love, that you'd married a man who wasn't me.

"There was a long period where I hated your husband. The harder he tried to be nice to me, the more I froze in his company and stayed completely away. My jealousy knew no bounds. I was painfully immature. It's no wonder you thought me too young for you.

"It wasn't until I heard he was dying that I stopped pitying myself and started thinking about what the two of you had to be going through.

"After he died, you never came around when I was at the house. When the family visited me in Carlsbad, you weren't with them. I wanted to see you, talk to you.

"Life was never the same for me after your marriage. I missed you desperately. But I was afraid that in those intervening years you'd lost any feelings you'd once had for me, whatever they were.

"When that accident happened to me, I looked at it as a godsend. I thought if I could engage your nursing services, I would discover that I'd grown beyond you and was no longer attracted.

"I had to find out if I'd been hanging on to an illusion without substance. If that was the case, I could finally let you go. I wanted out of prison, Michelle.

"Dear Lord—all it took was seeing you in the hall with Lynette and I knew those prison bars were never going to open for me.''

His head reared back. "So now I'm faced with the

gravest dilemma of my life. We're both members of the same family. There's no way I can avoid you.

"Help me, Michelle." He sounded like a man going down for the third time. "How do I tear you out of my heart? How does a person do that?"

CHAPTER TEN

SHE lifted her tremulous gaze to his. "I don't want you to tear me out. I plan to stay in there permanently. I want to be your wife. It's what I've wanted since I came to Carlsbad to nurse you."

"What did you say?"

Michelle had seen people in shock and recognized the signs.

Her hand went to her throat. "We do go back a long way, Zak. The aloof nine year old who tugged at my heartstrings grew into an engaging teen who was more fun to be with than anyone else I knew.

"The compassionate older Zak who came to the funeral to comfort me, reminded me how easy it was to talk to him, to share confidences.

"The Zak I've been living with day and night since the accident has come to mean something much more to me. In two weeks, you've taken my heart over completely. I'm in love with you, Zak. I admit it. It's the painful, all consuming kind of love that's never going to go away."

"Michelle—"

"Don't come near me yet, darling. Let me finish this while I can, and then we'll never have to talk about it again."

In a lightning moment, Zak's whole countenance underwent a transformation. The man standing a few feet away from her looked like someone who'd just been freed from an earthly trial. His handsome features relaxed. His body filled with new energy. In the depths of his eyes blazed a new green light.

"I loved Rob very much. He reminded me of Dad. I knew I'd never meet a better man. We had a wonderful marriage in the beginning. But when he was diagnosed with a fatal disease, he changed into a different man. He closed up on me and wouldn't let me help him.

"The last year of our marriage, I not only grieved because of his condition, but for the damaged state of our marriage. He was too proud to show me his vulnerability. It had the effect of distancing us from each other.

"When you came to the funeral, it would have been so easy to cry on your shoulder, Zak. The fact that I wanted to be with you and cry on your shoulder made me feel so guilty, it was like a betrayal of my love for Rob."

"Darling—"

"That guilt kept me from coming around you and the family. I eventually dated other men, most recently, Mike. Then you had that accident. What happened when I saw you at Sherilyn's is hard to describe.

"I felt this intense attraction to you. I couldn't believe it. It was overwhelming. Before I knew it, I realized I was in love with a man I believed was forbidden to me."

Zak made a sound in his throat that signaled so many emotions. Grief. Joy. Regret. Incredulity.

"In a way the last two years have been therapeutic for me because I've been able to help people who didn't shut me out. When I saw Mike Francis falling into the same kind of depression as Rob's, I refused to let it happen a second time.

"Because I fought so hard for him to be open with me, Mike let go of that pride and we became more than nurse and patient. We were both trying to find our way after a dark period in our lives. Consequently we leaned on each other. But he still had feelings for his ex-wife, and I wasn't at all sure I could give enough to our relationship to try and make it work.

"Then I saw you again. These weeks with you—" She tried to catch her breath, but couldn't.

"Does this mean you're going to marry me the second we can get the license?"

"Yes, darling."

"That's all I needed to hear." In a few strides he reached the sliding door and opened it and the screen. "Come with me. Our family's out walking along the surf. Let's tell them our news before we have to leave for the doctor."

She gravitated toward him. He cupped her face in his hands and gave her a kiss to die for. When he finally tore his lips from hers, he grasped her hand and led her toward an ocean more green than blue because the fog was still burning off.

The three people they loved had their backs to them. They were a good city block ahead.

"Sherilyn—Graham—" Zak called to them.

Three figures turned around.

"Wait up!" There was a look of joy on his face Michelle would treasure all her life.

He tightened his grip on her hand and they ran like children in the family's direction.

Suddenly Graham came sprinting toward them. Sherilyn wasn't far behind.

"You told him yes—" was all her brother said when he was close enough to stare into Michelle's eyes.

"Oh, yes!" she cried for happiness.

"Thank God!" He swung her around like a crazy man, then gave Zak a fierce hug her husband-to-be reciprocated with equal ferocity.

By this time Sherilyn, whose face radiated happiness, was hugging Michelle. Within seconds she broke down sobbing uncontrollably.

"What's going on?"

Zak put his arm around Lynette's shoulders and gave her a kiss on the forehead.

"Michelle and I are getting married."

She eyed him for a long moment. "I *knew* you two were in love with each other." Instead of anger or shock or resentment, Michelle saw sadness enter her niece's eyes. "I guess this means you'll both be moving away soon."

"Wrong, Lynette."

Zak's piercing gaze took in everyone as he slid his arm around Michelle's shoulders and pulled her tightly against him.

"We'll be living right here in Carlsbad for the rest of our lives. Why would I leave the family I love? We're planning on having a baby as soon as possible. That means we're going to need you guys more than ever."

There was a distinct tremor in his voice.

He couldn't have said anything guaranteed to bring the family greater joy.

Michelle wrapped her arm around his waist. One day

soon she'd tell her brother and sister-in-law the wonderful things Zak had told her in private. Things that would bring contentment and peace to their hearts.

Sherilyn clung to her brother. "It looks like there's going to be a wedding at the Sadler home. We'd better call the pastor and reserve the church."

His gaze trapped Michelle's. "Darling? What do you say we go inside the condo and start making plans."

Graham looped his arm around his daughter. "I'll call my secretary and tell her I won't be coming in today."

Lynette frowned. "How will I get to work?"

"That's all right. You can take my car," Michelle offered.

"I've got a better idea," Zak broke in. "After Michelle and I are through at the doctor's, we'll stop by the passport office and then drive to Riverside. That way we can all be together."

"Are you going to Greece before you get married?"

Zak smiled down at his niece. "No. Greece is our honeymoon destination. I told Nick that if I went there to meet my relatives, I'd be bringing my bride with me."

Michelle almost fainted from the thrill of hearing that news.

"That's why I want to get my application pushed through in record time."

He turned to Michelle. Beneath half-closed lids his eyes were glazed over with desire. "I've had to wait too long for this woman I've loved forever. I'm through wasting precious time."

"Amen," Graham said, clearing his throat. "Who wants waffles for breakfast?"

"You said that so I'd make them," Lynette muttered, but she was all smiles.

"Am I that transparent?"

"Yes!" everyone exclaimed at the same time.

The five of them strolled back to the condo. Twice Zak held Michelle back to suffocate her with kisses.

She never remembered her feet touching the sand.

EPILOGUE

Nisiros, Greece. One year later.

THERE was a knock on the door. "Kyrie Sadler? Your father wants to know if he and Anna can take your baby to the village with them. They won't be too long."

"Shall we let them dote on our little Caroline for another hour?" he murmured against Michelle's lips.

"Yes," she whispered honestly.

After making love since early morning, a heavy languor had stolen over her, holding her in its thrall. She had no inclination to move out of her husband's strong arms.

"I'm glad you said that." He turned his head toward the door. "Tell my father it's fine. We'll see them all later."

"Your family's going to think we're horrible."

"My father's so happy we've let him get to know his little golden haired granddaughter, he never wants us to leave."

"I don't want to go."

"That makes two of us. I blame you my darling wife for having turned me into a hedonist," he teased. "Father understands these things. That's why he and the family have left us alone. Again."

Zak's eyes ate her alive as they played over her face made rosy from the rasp of his jaw. His look was so sensual, a blush swept over her quickened body in response.

With a little moan of need, she slid her arm around his neck and kissed the male mouth she craved.

"I'll never be able to get enough of you," she said with a sigh some time later. "Even while I have you right here where I want you, even while I'm tasting you to my heart's content, I want more," her voice quavered. "No woman alive could love her husband more than I love you, Zak."

"No husband ever felt more loved," he murmured against her throat.

Her fingers toyed with the tendrils of black hair that had a tendency to curl against his bronzed neck. "If we didn't already have paradise to go home to, you'd never get me out of this bed or this room."

From their window in the Zannis villa on the island of Nisiros, they could look down on the adorable white village of Pali to the blue sea below.

"Now I understand why even as a boy, you loved the ocean so much you had to live where you could see it every day. If things had been different, you would have spent a great deal of your life growing up here."

Zak pulled her on top of him. Staring deeply into her eyes he said, "The gods have been kind and have allowed our firstborn to romp in this glorious backyard. I hope you realize that over the years our daughter is going to be spoiled rotten with these visits to see her grampa."

"I want another baby, Zak. She needs a little sister or brother so she'll learn to share. I'm praying that next time it will be a son with black hair like yours."

His beautiful white smile took her breath. "I've been

doing everything in my power to make that happen on this trip. Never has a husband been given a more delightful task. On a scale of one to ten, how am I faring so far?''

Liquid filled her eyes, intensifying the blue Zak had always likened to the pansies he'd once helped Sherilyn plant. Each one had a face and were her favorite flowers.

''You're off the chart and you know it—'' her voice shook. ''I've never known this kind of happiness in my life. You make me feel…immortal.''

His chest rose and fell heavily. ''That's how I feel whenever you touch me. Like I'm able to do anything, be anything. It's all because of you, Michelle. You're my very life.''

They were both out of breath as their mouths fused and caught fire. Once again they were consumed in a ritual of ecstasy as old as time itself.

The world fell away until they heard the whir of rotors hovering over the villa. At the unmistakable sound of modern civilization, they both let out a groan and unwillingly surfaced.

The helicopter had arrived from Kos.

Too soon they'd be leaving Greece for New York where they were going to spend a few days with Zak's mother's family. Everyone wanted to meet their little green eyed, three month old baby who was rumored to look a lot like her grandmother Caroline.

''Darling?'' he called to her softly.

''Yes?'' She raised eyes to him still glazed from their lovemaking.

''There's one thing we need to discuss before we leave this room.''

Her heart turned over. "What is it?"

"I know you're in a hurry to have one more baby. But if it doesn't happen, we can still adopt a child so Caroline has a sibling to grow up with. As soon as we get back to Carlsbad, let's start the application process. It'll be our insurance policy in case there's a problem."

He caught her cheek gently between his fingers. "I may not be a doctor, but it's common knowledge that it helps to be relaxed so conception can occur.

"Making love with you is too wonderful to let anything detract from our joy. What will be, will be."

Humbled by his wisdom, she reached for his hand to kiss the palm. "I've never loved you more than I love you at this moment. I need you, Zak. I've always needed you. You'll never know how much."

His eyes filmed over. "I *do* know. It's radiating from the depth of your soul. Since marrying you, my life is complete. Hold me, darling," he cried. "Never let me go."

"Never," she promised, rocking him in her arms.

Michelle had held him like this before. The pattern had been established long ago. She expected she'd be doing this until they both drew their last breath, and even beyond.

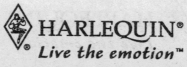

It's romantic comedy with a kick
(in a pair of strappy pink heels)!

Introducing

HARLEQUIN®

flipside

"It's chick-lit with the romance and happily-ever-
after ending that Harlequin is known for."
—*USA TODAY* bestselling author Millie Criswell,
author of *Staying Single*, October 2003

"Even though our heroine may take a few
false steps while finding her way, she does it
with wit and humor."
—Dorien Kelly, author of *Do-Over*,
November 2003

Launching October 2003.
Make sure you pick one up!

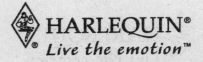

HARLEQUIN®
Live the emotion™

Visit us at www.harlequinflipside.com

HFGENERIC

If you enjoyed what you just read,
then we've got an offer you can't resist!

Take 2 bestselling love stories FREE!

Plus get a FREE surprise gift!

Clip this page and mail it to Harlequin Reader Service®

IN U.S.A.	IN CANADA
3010 Walden Ave.	P.O. Box 609
P.O. Box 1867	Fort Erie, Ontario
Buffalo, N.Y. 14240-1867	L2A 5X3

YES! Please send me 2 free Harlequin Romance® novels and my free surprise gift. After receiving them, if I don't wish to receive anymore, I can return the shipping statement marked cancel. If I don't cancel, I will receive 6 brand-new novels every month, before they're available in stores! In the U.S.A., bill me at the bargain price of $3.34 plus 25¢ shipping & handling per book and applicable sales tax, if any*. In Canada, bill me at the bargain price of $3.80 plus 25¢ shipping & handling per book and applicable taxes**. That's the complete price and a savings of 10% off the cover prices—what a great deal! I understand that accepting the 2 free books and gift places me under no obligation ever to buy any books. I can always return a shipment and cancel at any time. Even if I never buy another book from Harlequin, the 2 free books and gift are mine to keep forever.

186 HDN DNTX
386 HDN DNTY

Name _____ (PLEASE PRINT)

Address _____ Apt.# _____

City _____ State/Prov. _____ Zip/Postal Code _____

* Terms and prices subject to change without notice. Sales tax applicable in N.Y.
** Canadian residents will be charged applicable provincial taxes and GST.
All orders subject to approval. Offer limited to one per household and not valid to current Harlequin Romance® subscribers.
® are registered trademarks of Harlequin Enterprises Limited.

HROM02   ©2001 Harlequin Enterprises Limited

Is your man too good to be true?

Hot, gorgeous AND romantic?
If so, he could be a Harlequin® Blaze™ series cover model!

Our grand-prize winners will receive a trip for two to New York City to shoot the cover of a Blaze novel, and will stay at the luxurious Plaza Hotel.
Plus, they'll receive $500 U.S. spending money!
The runner-up winners will receive $200 U.S.
to spend on a romantic dinner for two.

It's easy to enter!

In 100 words or less, tell us what makes your boyfriend or spouse a true romantic and the perfect candidate for the cover of a Blaze novel, and include in your submission two photos of this potential cover model.

All entries must include the written submission of the contest entrant, two photographs of the model candidate and the Official Entry Form and Publicity Release forms completed in full and signed by both the model candidate and the contest entrant. Harlequin, along with the experts at Elite Model Management, will select a winner.

For photo and complete Contest details, please refer to the Official Rules on the next page. All entries will become the property of Harlequin Enterprises Ltd. and are not returnable.

Please visit www.blazecovermodel.com to download a copy of the Official Entry Form and Publicity Release Form or send a request to one of the addresses below.

Please mail your entry to: **Harlequin Blaze Cover Model Search**

In U.S.A.
P.O. Box 9069
Buffalo, NY
14269-9069

In Canada
P.O. Box 637
Fort Erie, ON
L2A 5X3

No purchase necessary. Contest open to Canadian and U.S. residents who are 18 and over.
Void where prohibited. Contest closes September 30, 2003.

HBCVRMODEL1

HARLEQUIN BLAZE COVER MODEL SEARCH CONTEST 3569 OFFICIAL RULES
NO PURCHASE NECESSARY TO ENTER

1. To enter, submit two (2) 4" x 6" photographs of a boyfriend or spouse (who must be 18 years of age or older) taken no later than three (3) months from the time of entry: a close-up, waist up, shirtless photograph; and a fully clothed, full-length photograph, then, tell us, in 100 words or fewer, why he should be a Harlequin Blaze cover model and how he is romantic. Your complete "entry" must include: (i) your essay, (ii) the Official Entry Form and Publicity Release Form printed below completed and signed by you (as "Entrant"), (iii) the photographs (with your hand-written name, address and phone number, and your model's name, address and phone number on the back of each photograph), and (iv) the Publicity Release Form and Photograph Representation Form printed below completed and signed by your model (as "Model"), and should be sent via first-class mail to either: Harlequin Blaze Cover Model Search Contest 3569, P.O. Box 9069, Buffalo, NY, 14269-9069, or Harlequin Blaze Cover Model Search Contest 3569, P.O. Box 637, Fort Erie, Ontario L2A 5X3. All submissions must be in English and be received no later than September 30, 2003. Limit: one entry per person, household or organization. **Purchase or acceptance of a product offer does not improve your chances of winning.** All entry requirements must be strictly adhered to for eligibility and to ensure fairness among entries.

2. Ten (10) Finalist submissions (photographs and essays) will be selected by a panel of judges consisting of members of the Harlequin editorial, marketing and public relations staff, as well as a representative from Elite Model Management (Toronto) Inc., based on the following criteria:

Aptness/Appropriateness of submitted photographs for a Harlequin Blaze cover—70%
Originality of Essay—20%
Sincerity of Essay—10%

In the event of a tie, duplicate finalists will be selected. The photographs submitted by finalists will be posted on the Harlequin website no later than November 15, 2003 (at www.blazecovermodel.com), and viewers may vote, in rank order, on their favorite(s) to assist in the panel of judges' final determination of the Grand Prize and Runner-up winning entries based on the above judging criteria. All decisions of the judges are final.

3. All entries become the property of Harlequin Enterprises Ltd. and none will be returned. Any entry may be used for future promotional purposes. Elite Model Management (Toronto) Inc. and/or its partners, subsidiaries and affiliates operating as "Elite Model Management" will have access to all entries including all personal information, and may contact any Entrant and/or Model in its sole discretion for their own business purposes. Harlequin and Elite Model Management (Toronto) Inc. are separate entities with no legal association or partnership whatsoever having no power to bind or obligate the other or create any expressed or implied obligation or responsibility on behalf of the other, such that Harlequin shall not be responsible in any way for any acts or omissions of Elite Model Management (Toronto) Inc. or its partners, subsidiaries and affiliates in connection with the Contest or otherwise and Elite Model Management shall not be responsible in any way for any acts or omissions of Harlequin or its partners, subsidiaries and affiliates in connection with the contest or otherwise.

4. All Entrants and Models must be residents of the U.S. or Canada, be 18 years of age or older, and have no prior criminal convictions. The contest is not open to any Model that is a professional model and/or actor in any capacity at the time of the entry. Contest void wherever prohibited by law; all applicable laws and regulations apply. Any litigation within the Province of Quebec regarding the conduct or organization of a publicity contest may be submitted to the Régie des alcools, des courses et des jeux for a ruling, and any litigation regarding the awarding of a prize may be submitted to the Régie only for the purpose of helping the parties reach a settlement. Employees and immediate family members of Harlequin Enterprises Ltd., D.L. Blair, Inc., Elite Model Management (Toronto) Inc. and their parents, affiliates, subsidiaries and all other agencies, entities and persons connected with the use, marketing or conduct of this Contest are not eligible to enter. Acceptance of any prize offered constitutes permission to use Entrants' and Models' names, essay submissions, photographs or other likenesses for the purposes of advertising, trade, publication and promotion on behalf of Harlequin Enterprises Ltd., its parent, affiliates, subsidiaries, assigns and other authorized entities involved in the judging and promotion of the contest without further compensation to any Entrant or Model, unless prohibited by law.

5. Finalists will be determined no later than October 30, 2003. Prize Winners will be determined no later than January 31, 2004. Grand Prize Winners (consisting of winning Entrant and Model) will be required to sign and return Affidavit of Eligibility/Release of Liability and Model Release forms within thirty (30) days of notification. Non-compliance with this requirement and within the specified time period will result in disqualification and an alternate will be selected. Any prize notification returned as undeliverable will result in the awarding of the prize to an alternate set of winners. All travelers (or parent/legal guardian of a minor) must execute the Affidavit of Eligibility/Release of Liability prior to ticketing and must possess required travel documents (e.g. valid photo ID) where applicable. Travel dates sponsored by Sponsor but no later than May 30, 2004.

6. Prizes: One (1) Grand Prize—the opportunity for the Model to appear on the cover of a paperback book from the Harlequin Blaze series, and a 3 day/2 night trip for two (Entrant and Model) to New York, NY for the photo shoot of Model which includes round-trip coach air transportation from the commercial airport nearest the winning Entrant's home to New York, NY, (or, in lieu of air transportation, $100 cash payable to Entrant and Model, if the winning Entrant's home is within 250 miles of New York, NY), hotel accommodations (double occupancy) at the Plaza Hotel and $500 cash spending money payable to Entrant and Model, (approximate prize value: $8,000), and one (1) Runner-up Prize of $200 cash payable to Entrant and Model for a romantic dinner for two (approximate prize value: $200). Prizes are valued in U.S. currency. Prizes consist of only those items listed as part of the prize. No substitution of prize(s) permitted by winners. All prizes are awarded jointly to the Entrant and Model of the winning entries, and are not severable - prizes and obligations may not be assigned or transferred. Any change to the Entrant and/or Model of the winning entries will result in disqualification and an alternate will be selected. Taxes on prize are the sole responsibility of winners. Any and all expenses and/or items not specifically described as part of the prize are the sole responsibility of winners. Harlequin Enterprises Ltd. and D.L. Blair, Inc., their parents, affiliates, and subsidiaries are not responsible for errors in printing of Contest entries and/or game pieces. No responsibility is assumed for lost, stolen, late, illegible, incomplete, inaccurate, non-delivered, postage due or misdirected mail or entries. In the event of printing or other errors which may result in unintended prize values or duplication of prizes, all affected game pieces or entries shall be null and void.

7. Winners will be notified by mail. For winners' list (available after March 31, 2004), send a self-addressed, stamped envelope to: Harlequin Blaze Cover Model Search Contest 3569 Winners, P.O. Box 4200, Blair, NE 68009-4200, or refer to the Harlequin website (at www.blazecovermodel.com).

Contest sponsored by Harlequin Enterprises Ltd., P.O. Box 9042, Buffalo, NY 14269-9042.

Your opinion is important to us! Please take a few moments to share your thoughts with us about your experiences with Harlequin and Silhouette books. Your comments will be very useful in ensuring that we deliver books you love to read.
Please take a few minutes to complete the questionnaire, then send it to us at the address below.

Send your completed questionnaires to:
Harlequin/Silhouette Reader Survey, P.O. Box 9046, Buffalo, NY 14269-9046

1. As you may know, there are many different lines under the Harlequin and Silhouette brands. Each of the lines is listed below. Please check the box that most represents your reading habit for each line.

Line	Currently read this line	Do not read this line	Not sure if I read this line
Harlequin American Romance	❑	❑	❑
Harlequin Duets	❑	❑	❑
Harlequin Romance	❑	❑	❑
Harlequin Historicals	❑	❑	❑
Harlequin Superromance	❑	❑	❑
Harlequin Intrigue	❑	❑	❑
Harlequin Presents	❑	❑	❑
Harlequin Temptation	❑	❑	❑
Harlequin Blaze	❑	❑	❑
Silhouette Special Edition	❑	❑	❑
Silhouette Romance	❑	❑	❑
Silhouette Intimate Moments	❑	❑	❑
Silhouette Desire	❑	❑	❑

2. Which of the following best describes why you bought *this book?* One answer only, please.

the picture on the cover	❑	the title	❑
the author	❑	the line is one I read often	❑
part of a miniseries	❑	saw an ad in another book	❑
saw an ad in a magazine/newsletter	❑	a friend told me about it	❑
I borrowed/was given this book	❑	other:	❑

3. Where did you buy *this book?* One answer only, please.

at Barnes & Noble	❑	at a grocery store	❑
at Waldenbooks	❑	at a drugstore	❑
at Borders	❑	on eHarlequin.com Web site	❑
at another bookstore	❑	from another Web site	❑
at Wal-Mart	❑	Harlequin/Silhouette Reader	❑
at Target	❑	Service/through the mail	
at Kmart	❑	used books from anywhere	❑
at another department store or mass merchandiser	❑	I borrowed/was given this book	❑

4. On average, how many Harlequin and Silhouette books do you buy at one time?

I buy _____ books at one time	❑
I rarely buy a book	❑

MRQ403HR-1A

5. How many times per month do you shop for any *Harlequin and/or Silhouette* books?
One answer only, please.

1 or more times a week	❏	a few times per year	❏
1 to 3 times per month	❏	less often than once a year	❏
1 to 2 times every 3 months	❏	never	❏

6. When you think of your ideal heroine, which *one* statement describes her the best?
One answer only, please.

She's a woman who is strong-willed	❏	She's a desirable woman	❏
She's a woman who is needed by others	❏	She's a powerful woman	❏
She's a woman who is taken care of	❏	She's a passionate woman	❏
She's an adventurous woman		She's a sensitive woman	❏

7. The following statements describe types or genres of books that you may be
interested in reading. Pick *up to 2 types* of books that you are most interested in.

I like to read about truly romantic relationships	❏
I like to read stories that are sexy romances	❏
I like to read romantic comedies	❏
I like to read a romantic mystery/suspense	❏
I like to read about romantic adventures	❏
I like to read romance stories that involve family	❏
I like to read about a romance in times or places that I have never seen	❏
Other: _____	❏

*The following questions help us to group your answers with those readers who are
similar to you. Your answers will remain confidential.*

8. Please record your year of birth below.

19 _____

9. What is your marital status?

single ❏   married ❏   common-law ❏   widowed ❏
divorced/separated ❏

10. Do you have children 18 years of age or younger currently living at home?

yes ❏   no ❏

11. Which of the following best describes your employment status?

employed full-time or part-time ❏   homemaker ❏   student ❏
retired ❏   unemployed ❏

12. Do you have access to the Internet from either home or work?

yes ❏   no ❏

13. Have you ever visited eHarlequin.com?

yes ❏   no ❏

14. What state do you live in?

_____

15. Are you a member of Harlequin/Silhouette Reader Service?

yes ❏   Account # _____   no ❏   MRQ403HR-1B

Witchcraft, deceit and more...
all FREE from

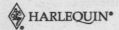